FAEDRA ROSE

EVERNIGHT PUBLISHING ®

www.evernightpublishing.com

FAEDRA ROSE

SINISTER DESIRES

Loving Monsters, 1

Faedra Rose

Copyright © 2022

Chapter One

Flicking up the collar of my leather jacket, I adjust my scarf to protect my neck from the bitter chill. The one downside of having a funky neon orange pixie cut during fall—a bare neck. Breathing into my gloved hands for extra warmth, I watch as my escaping breath mists in the air before whorling away on the breeze.

The blood moon of All Hallows' Eve hangs high overhead, its lurid radiance obscured by the twisting and gnarled branches of the woods. A piercing screech in the night disturbs a colony of bats and they take to the sky, their small silhouettes dancing chaotically past the moon.

I could kick myself for my current predicament; not that I mind the dark or solitude. But what kind of idiot gives her ex a second chance? Tonight, we were meant to just hang out, drive around town trick-or-treating like old times, and then we were going to take our ill-gotten gains to The Lookout and enjoy sexy Halloween fun in the backseat…

I should have known it was a trick. Jerks don't change their colors. So instead of rekindling our college romance, he thought humiliating me in front of all the other couples at The Lookout would be a spectacularly funny way to wrap up our sham of a date. The fucker took my candy, then kicked me out of the car, leaving me alone and with no way of getting home.

I could fucking scream. The next time I see Cooper, it's going to be the last time he has functional balls—and I'm not talking about the ones he plays gridiron with! *Ugh.* So, now, here I am, walking for miles through the woods that back onto all the old farms in the region. Some still have elderly caretakers, but most are derelict and abandoned—left to rot and ruin after the last generation of farmers passed on.

Farrowville doesn't have space in its heart for people like me. Like most of Iowa, it's a town full of Midwestern born and bred families. They go to church, follow sports, and give casseroles to new neighbors. Nothing ever changes here, and everyone knows everyone else. There's no place for a bold, gothic artist with dreams of making a difference in the world. I got out of this hole as soon as I could, my salvation coming in the form of an acceptance to an esteemed arts college just out of state.

But, like so many others, I don't have the heart to entirely divorce myself of my family. We might not gel on all things, but my folks have supported my dreams, as unconventional as they have always been. And I don't hate seeing my siblings. Yes. Plural. All five of them. Out of the lot, I'm the ugly duckling, the fish out of water—

the one that has just never fit in. Despite that, we get along in our own strange way.

So that's why I'm back here on familiar turf again to begin with. I'm home for the holidays, paying my expected familial dues. Playing nice with my brothers and sisters, sharing stories over piss-flavored cider, and gathering around our old twelve-seater table for Mom's famous spiced pumpkin pie. Mom'll be upset that I didn't call them for a lift, but I'm not a little girl anymore, and I think sometimes she forgets that. At twenty-three I may be the youngest of the Llewellyns, but I pride myself on my independence.

I purse my lips as the temperature seems to drop the deeper into the woods I go. It makes sense. The microclimate of the dell and the trees would hold the moisture and cool in, trapping the rising damp of the earth. All the same, it sets my nerves on edge, and my heart races. I love superstition, and I love nothing more than the thrill of being afraid. It's why I gravitated toward the goth lifestyle and why I enjoy risk-taking.

Life is meant to be lived, and if the world's going to be a bitch and scare the crap out of you from time to time, you might as well learn to revel in it! I grin despite myself and allow my imagination to run wild, viewing the woods through new eyes. Shadows loom, stretching their long, crooked fingers across the dark, leaf-littered ground, and I wonder—*what if the trees were sentient beings? What if on Halloween their spirits break free of their bark-covered shells to roam free?*

I snicker, my black boots squelching through the seasonal puddles underfoot. A long, mournful howl breaks the night's intrepid silence, and my voice catches in my throat as I come to a stand-still. Eyes wide, I hug myself, alertness thrumming through every fiber of my body like fire. *I didn't think of the wolves...* I realize. *And*

I'm completely unarmed. I don't even have keys on me, just my phone.

A second howl joins the first, and the hairs on the back of my neck prickle. Licking my chapped lips, I swallow the sour bile that threatens to rise up my throat. Dancing with danger is one thing, but being torn apart—alive—by hungry wolves? *Not my idea of fun.* Picking up my pace, I set off into the darkness, following the worn trail through the trees toward home.

There're still a few miles between me and the family farm, and I know I can't outrun wolves; nor can I run with them, though all those feminist quotes would have you believe otherwise. My only hope is that they decide I'm not worth the effort. *Goddammit.* With my generous curves, maybe there's no hope at all? Truth is, I'd probably make a great meal for half a dozen ravenous wolves. Mom always says fat equals flavor! Ugh. The irony.

Mist rolls in, filling the dell and obscuring everything below my knees. "Shit," I breathe. There are bound to be obstacles on the old path, and now I'm not going to be able to see them until it's too late. Howls fill the woods, one, two, three ... maybe six or seven? I'm not sure. And then I hear the sound of padded footfalls in the darkness. *They're flanking me, getting ready for the take-down.* Heart thundering in my chest, I'm all out of options.

Pumping my arms for all I'm worth, I sprint headlong into the shadows. With my pulse thumping in my ears, all I can hear, now, is the sound of my own labored breathing and the occasional drawn-out howl as the wolves close in.

I'm not ready to die! I cry out in my mind—to God, the universe, my foremothers, or All Hallows' spirits; I can't be sure. Everything that has previously existed in my life has narrowed down to one imperative goal: survive. Heart set on home, I push myself until my lungs are burning and a pain flares in my side, stealing the breath from me. I gasp out in pain, my hand finding the confluence of my hip. *A fucking stitch! You've got to be kidding me. Not. Now!*

But in the next second, the stitch is the least of my problems. Something catches my boot, and suddenly I'm airborne. A scream rips from my throat as I fly for what seems like forever. I hit the sodden ground hard and shriek as pain radiates through me from my chest. My ankle feels like it's at entirely the wrong angle.

"Fuck!" I sob, drawing myself up onto my knees. Reaching out for something, anything, with which to support myself, I find a large crooked stick. Gritting my teeth, I mutter a string of profanities under my breath as I clutch it with both hands, pulling myself up by sheer force of will. A low growl rumbles behind me, and I forget how to breathe. *This is it. This is where I make my stand. This is where I die—in the woods on Halloween. Fucking perfect.* A ridiculously nervous, bordering on maniacal laugh escapes me as I turn to face the wolf.

"All right, bitch," I say, raising the stick like a baseball bat. "Let's do this. If I'm going to die, you're going to be chewing on my fat ass with one mother fucker of a headache!"

The wolf growls again, baring its fangs in a vicious snarl of warning.

"Come on!" I goad. "What are you waiting for?"

The wolf lowers its head, pawing at the earth as it gets ready to launch.

No. Fuck you! And then, committing my weight to the swing, I lash out first, bringing the stick around in a wide arc. I catch the side of the wolf's face, and it seems as though the moment plays out in slow motion. I see the wolf's flesh ripple with the impact of my blow, and its nose scrunch as the force knocks its head to the side—causing it to stumble and yelp.

"Come on! Is that all you've got? Where are your friends?" I shout, trying to ignore the searing pain in my ankle. I gingerly put weight on it, struggling to keep my balance. The wolf growls again, and its pack stalks from the darkness. "All right, now this is a party!" I scream at them, gripping the stick tight. *If I'm going down, I'm going down swinging!*

The wolves' golden eyes glimmer in the moonlight like jewels. *They're such beautiful beasts. If only they weren't trying to eat me...* A brisk breeze ruffles my hair, and the air behind me chills so suddenly, and unexpectedly, that it feels like some cruel trickster has snuck up on me and tipped a bucket of ice-water down my spine. I freeze in place as the wolves whine. One after the other, they back-step, their glittering eyes focused somewhere behind me. Then the wolves flee as one, turning on their heels, deciding that I'm not worth standing up to whomever—or whatever—lurks at my back, bringing the chill of the grave with it.

Trembling, I will myself to turn and face my unexpected savior. *Or is it damnation?* Agonizingly slowly I find the courage to pivot around. Eyes on the ground, my gaze travels up a weathered black trench coat which whispers eerily in the mist as if it's alive, like sentient, breathing shadows. I swallow the bile that creeps up my throat, daring to look higher still.

An imposing figure reveals broad shoulders, and upon those intimidating shoulders sits a pumpkin—a jack-O-lantern to be exact. With the most menacing, soul-sapping, sharp-toothed grin, and angled, hollowed-out eyes that burn not with the innocent flames of tea-light candles, but with the fucking fires of Hell. I open my mouth to scream, but no sound escapes. Not even a squeak. My lips move, but my lungs fail me.

The jack-O-lantern opens its coat with long, green, provocatively clawed fingers to reveal an equally moss-green body; the body of a man, but not. My unblinking gaze trails down solid pecs to find a ridiculously ripped set of abs ... and then... *Sweet mother of God!* This abomination is packing the biggest, thickest cock I've ever seen. *It must be twelve inches! And it's green, too!*

I can't do anything but stare, immobile as the monster steps closer, its blazing eyes dancing with a terrifying intelligence. I gasp as a leafy vine creeps out from under his trench coat, trailing over the moist earth. Its delicate tendrils twist around my ankle, wrapping it up like a bandage of green gauze; then they tighten, and a cry bursts out of me at the sharp but fleeting pain that follows. I watch with rapt fascination as the vines uncoil, releasing my leg, only to disappear back beneath the jack-O-lantern's coat of darkness.

I instinctively twitch my ankle, then gasp, glancing up at the towering monster before testing my weight on it. "It doesn't hurt," I whisper in awe. "You fixed it?"

The jack-O-lantern tilts its pumpkin head the way a curious cat might, as if it wants to communicate.

"Thank you," I stammer, raising my voice above a whisper. "You saved me from those wolves, and now you've re-set my foot." I lick my lips nervously when no conversation is forthcoming. "Can you speak?"

The monster shakes its head slowly from side to side, never taking its burning eyes from me. It watches me for a time. Then another tendril snakes out, writhing toward me to seize my wrist, tightening just enough to hurt. It tugs, drawing me nearer and nearer. I stumble forward, eyes wide, my heart in my throat as the living pumpkin vines pull my gloved hand toward its monstrous, green, dark-veined cock.

I know I should pull back, but I'm mesmerized. *Oh, what the absolute fuck, Charleigh? You want to touch it?* I bite my inner lip as my fingers come to hover just above its heinously impressive length. I don't know what to say or what to think. And then the words tumble from my lips before I can make sense of them. "You did save me…" I reason. If it had wanted to kill me, it would have done so already. If the monster just wants a little tug of gratitude, what's the harm?

"You're not going to kill me, are you?" I ask plaintively, my dark eyes searching the Hellfire in his. "I'm going to touch you now…" I say, as much to myself as to the jack-O-lantern. Licking my lips, I take a deep breath and allow the tips of my fingers to trail along its cock. *It's warm.* Not what I was expecting at all. The tendril on my wrist eases its grasp the more I cautiously explore.

In the next instant, its long fingers are on both my shoulders, pushing me down. *Oh, God. It wants a fucking blowjob!* I'm alone in the woods on All Hallows' Eve, unarmed, and a monster is forcefully guiding me to my knees. And I have to admit, I'm filled with no small amount of mortal horror, but I'm also disturbingly turned on. *I'll be the girl that not only met a monster, but also sucked one off! I don't think it gets any more goth than that.*

"All right," I say. "Have it your way."

The jack-O-lantern removes its hands as I kneel on the damp ground and wrap one hand around its pulsing green cock. Glancing up into its fiery eyes once more, I hold out my tongue, leaning forward, and cautiously lick the gleaming green tip. I recoil as its slick juices touch my tongue, assaulting my tastebuds. I can't believe it. There are no words. *Its pre-cum tastes like fucking candy!* "Holy shit." I can't help the deviously sly and excited smile that curves my lips as I go in for another taste.

Chapter Two

While his pre-cum tastes like candy, the green flesh of his cock tastes like oven-roasted pumpkin. It's sweet and savory all at once. The dark veins pulse rhythmically under my fingertips as I stroke the monster's cock and trail my tongue around its enormous, smooth head. *What is this creature?* I wonder. How can a beast be so inhuman and human at the same time? And why, for the love of God, why are my insides tingling?

The familiar ache of desire causes my cunt to throb, and I know in my gut that I need this nightmarish cock filling me as surely as I need air to live. The thought of its length and girth stretching and violating my very small but buxom human form has me clenching my thighs in angst. *I'm wet. Sweet God, what is wrong with me?* But I can't deny how I feel. And this monster ... this jack-O-lantern, has yet to harm me.

Perhaps I'll walk away from this encounter unscathed. Or perhaps, once it's had its way with me, it'll kill me. Maybe it'll burn me from within with its blazing Hellfire, immolating me alive? Or maybe it'll use those ghastly claws to rip my still-beating heart from my breast, and leave what remains of me for the wolves, after all? I can't know. And the truth is, after what happened earlier tonight with Cooper? *I don't fucking care.*

Maybe it's always been my destiny to fuck a monster? Maybe it's fate that everything has unfolded precisely as it has to bring me to this precise moment, here and now, blowing an urban legend in the middle of the woods on Halloween? My goth heart thrills at the ludicrously absurd idea. *Fuck it. Live or die, I'm doing this!*

Taking the monster's cock in both hands, I open wide, enveloping its head with the warmth of my mouth. Its slick sweetness coats my tongue as my lips stretch to accommodate such an ass-puckeringly huge dick. The jack-O-lantern groans as its cock hits the back of my throat. The sound is as unsettling as it is hot, and I feel inspired to take the beast as deep as humanly possible. Soon, I feel the rake of claws through my hair, trailing lightly over my scalp. Then the monster takes a hold of my head, guiding me forward, encouraging me to take more and more.

As I relax my gag reflex, I relinquish my hold on his cock and allow the monster to use me as he wills. For it, I am a willing hole, and I want it to seek its dark pleasures in me. The monster inches forward, holding my head in a terrifying, vice-like grip while thrusting its green beast down my throat. In and out, again and again, the breathtaking cock is relentless in seeking the deepest depths it can reach, sometimes cutting off my air supply altogether. I gasp around it, the brisk night air filling my hungry lungs, my eyes watering.

It's so fucking big there is just no fitting it all in! I've deep-throated my fair share of college men, and even the biggest of them would feel my lips wrapped around their base, their firm balls slapping against my chin as they impatiently sought their own orgasm—with little regard for my own. The jack-O-lantern withdraws entirely then, his erect cock dripping more of that cloyingly sweet pre-cum. It releases my head and strokes my cheek with the back of its sinister curved claws, as if to say *good girl*. The strange, small measure of affection and praise makes my ego soar and my heart sing.

Catching my breath, I sit back on my heels, looking up at my very own nightmare. He's horrifying, but perfectly so, like a dark, twisted artwork brought to life. I lick my lips and moan. When did my hand slip under my dress and between my legs? All I know is that I'm horny as hell and sopping wet; my musk leaks down my thighs, sticky and warm.

The monster tilts its head in that cat-like manner again, then squats down before me. Using its claws, it delicately lifts the fabric of my Halloween-print dress and watches me furiously rubbing my clit. I can't believe how turned on I am by this grotesque, pumpkin-headed, black-clawed, tendril-wielding creature. It's curiosity and attentiveness have my cunt quivering with desire. And then I'm gushing, my release puddling between my legs on the dark, damp earth as I cry out. Head back, eyes closed, I ride the waves of my orgasm until I'm panting and light-headed.

I knew I was into all things taboo, but this is something else—it's literally otherworldly. *And I want more. I need more.* I want to cum for this monster until I'm bow-legged and spent, until I'm nothing more than a hot mess of a human fuck-bag filled with pumpkin seed. No longer caring about how I look, or anything at all to be perfectly honest, I sit back, then lay down on the leaf-littered ground. *I must look a sight!* A petite but curvy woman with a neon orange pixie cut, laying spread-legged on a carpet of fall-colored leaves. All sense of modesty long forgotten, a laugh escapes me, and I grin, my eyes finding the blood moon and the twinkling stars above.

Closing my eyes, I exhale and breathe deep, not thinking, just feeling. I drink in the moment, the scent of rot and decay in the woods, the petrichor of the swirling mist that dampens my bare skin with tiny droplets, like millions of reflective crystal balls. *I wonder what each one might reveal of my future if a fortune teller were to read them?* And then I feel a gentle caress on my inner thigh, and my breath hitches in my throat.

The jack-O-lantern crawls over me, its burning Hellfire flickering behind the sinister, cut-out eye slots as I feel more tendrils trailing over me. My breathing becomes heavy once more as suddenly my wrists and ankles are wrapped and bound, the warm vines securing me spread-eagle. Other tendrils emerge as I raise my head and watch in abject horror—and awe—as they snake out from under the trench coat of shadows and down between my legs, seeking my soft, wet, and tender places.

The monster supports himself on his clawed hands, and as his tendrils tickle my aching clit, he rests his pumpkin forehead to mine. Images assault my mind, like a living montage, and I see the truth of the jack-O-lantern. He was once a man named Jack, as human as I, but he was a trickster and hurt many souls with his malicious ways. Jealous of his reputation, the Devil wanted to claim his soul, but being quick and clever, Jack outwitted the Devil in a cunning deal.

Jack could never enter Heaven, nor, after many long years on Earth, could he find respite in Hell. Tired and lost in the darkness, the Devil eventually took pity on him and gave him his blazing pumpkin head, filled with the fires of Hell itself, so that he would have light wherever he went, for the rest of his lonely days.

I gasp as the monster—Jack—lifts his head back, his burning eyes boring holes into my very soul, and my heart aches for him. He is a cursed creature and has never had a chance at redemption. He's just caught in-between, damned to an eternal purgatory among billions of people he can never relate to or communicate with. *How cruel life can be...* An unbidden tear spills from my eye, and I sniffle it away. Reaching up with one hand, I lay it against the warm flesh of Jack's pumpkin head.

"Can this be undone?" I ask, staring into his

flames.

Jack shakes his head, and his tendrils increase their ministrations between my legs.

I bite my lip, drawing blood. "Oh, God," I moan, as one particularly thick vine finds its way inside of me. Its soft but rigid form fucks me, gently and slowly at first, but then with more fervor. I writhe against my bonds, grinding my ass into the dirt as pleasure wracks my body. "It's not fair," I sulk. "You make me feel so good, and you saved me." My engorged clit pulses in time with my heart, and I can barely stand it. "What do you want? What can I do for you?" I ask mid-moan, my voice escaping me in a breathy whisper.

Jack sits back on his knees, and I watch as he cradles his arms to his chest, then rocks them from side to side, as if nursing a baby.

My eyes widen at the realization, just as my second orgasm tears through me with brutal force, setting every nerve ablaze. I quiver and buck, whimpering through it. *I'm so tender now, and every part of me burns!* But it doesn't matter. Jack wants a baby, a legacy to share with the world—offspring to keep him company through his eternal exile from Heaven and Hell. *And I'm going to be the one to give that to him,* I decide. *God and Devil be damned. No one should be alone! No one. Not even Jack the Trickster.*

"I don't know how it's going to work," I breathe. "But yes. Fill me with your seed, Jack, and I'll give you the family you desire." I grin as the thought crosses my mind. "We can have our very own little pumpkin patch!"

Chapter Three

Something in the undergrowth rustles nearby, followed by the telltale sound of a twig snapping underfoot. Jack's entire bearing changes in an instant. He covers me with his body like a cat on all fours, his fiery eyes blazing. His many pumpkin vines and tendrils rise, some bursting through his coat—creating the illusion of wings—alive and ready to fight ... *to protect me.*

Silently, and carefully, so not as to alarm Jack, I roll over beneath him, my eyes searching the darkness for any sign of danger. I hear it again, and faster than lightning Jack moves as stealthily as a shadow, plunging into the woods. A second later a strangled scream pierces the night, and my brow furrows. *There's something strangely familiar about that voice...*

A body skids through the darkness, landing on the path several feet away. And in a shocking moment of recognition, I know who it is. *I'd recognize that blond mop of curls anywhere. It's Cooper.*

Cooper groans in pain and moves to lift his head, but then Jack's on him, plucking him from the earth by his neck, his claws wrapped tightly around his throat. My monster roars at my ex-boyfriend, though his menacing carved smile doesn't move. I hear the trickle of fluid on the earth as Cooper grasps uselessly at the giant hand choking him.

I look down, following the darkening trail on his jeans in the moonlight. *He's pissed himself. Gross.* And for half an instant, I'm surprised by my own callousness.

Once upon a time, we'd skipped stones down by the lake, and stolen bread from our folks to feed the wild ducks. We'd climbed trees, shared stories, mud-wrestled, and raced our bikes down long dirt roads, the colorful beads on our spokes clinking noisily as we went. Then we grew up, and that innocent childhood friendship suddenly became something more. We shared our first kiss in my tree-house and played hookie from Sunday school to enjoy heavy petting sessions down by the river.

A half-smile almost flits across my lips, but then I remember all the bad; the memories that are still painfully raw. The way he'd changed the older we got. How he'd grown aware of his man-candy good looks and transformed into an arrogant jock overnight. The way he flirted with other girls while we were still clearly together. And then the night he cheated on me comes roaring back with crystal clarity.

I'd found him balls deep in my dorm mate … my slender, blonde, cheerleader dorm mate, Cassidy. *I taught that bitch basic Biology! Ugh.* And his words from that night still ring clear as a bell in my mind, and still sting— even now. *"What're you looking at? It's over, Morticia. No one wants your freak ass."*

Why did I ever give him a second chance? I wonder, as I sit among the fall leaves, watching Cooper's urine-soiled legs flail hopelessly. Desperation? The need to feel loved? Validation? His pleas that he was a changed man, and that he'd realized how shallow and cruel he'd been? All of it, really, I guess. But now, I know the truth. After tonight's cruelty, I know that I mean nothing to him. He finds me so repugnant that he couldn't even follow through and fuck me before he dumped me. He just stole my candy and threw me out of the car like trash.

Anger resurges, hot and resentful. Rising to my feet, I brush myself off, straighten my dress, and approach Cooper, standing beside Jack. "This sorry excuse for a man used to be my lover, Jack," I say, unsure if the ancient monster would understand a more modern term like *boyfriend*. "And he's broken my heart, twice."

Jack growls in response, a deep rumble that seems to vibrate through the very earth, and he draws Cooper nearer, intimidating the poor simpleton with his fiery gaze.

"What are you doing out here, anyway, Cooper? Come to gloat? Maybe you thought you could take advantage and fuck me out-of-sight? You wouldn't want everyone seeing you—the shining jock—fucking around with the town goth, would you?"

Cooper chokes out something unintelligible.

I sigh. "Let him down, Jack. I want to hear whatever pathetic excuse he has to offer."

My monster drops Cooper like a sack of shit, and he hits the ground hard, grasping at his throat, gasping for air.

I give him a minute before pressing the matter. "So, why are you here in the woods, Coop? You left me for dead up at The Lookout."

My pitiful ex scrambles backward on his ass, his eyes full of terror as his gaze flits from me to Jack. "I always knew you were a freak," he spits, struggling to his feet. "Everyone was right about you; you're a fucking Devil worshiper, aren't you? And what the fuck is this? The demon you summoned to fuck?"

My laughter fills the night, and I bump into Jack as I cover my mouth to suppress my giggles, my eyes glistening with tears. "Oh, honey. No, no, no. The Devil's a bit of a jerk, really. I worship no one. I'm my own woman. And this? This beautiful beast of darkness is Jack. See, the difference between you—pretty boy—and my Jack, is that he actually wants a chance at redemption. He wants to bring a beautiful legacy into the world. You, on the other hand, you're just an immature shit who'll spend his days fucking over everyone you can. You'd play women like you play your sport. Then you'd no doubt become a corporate whore and a sell-out."

I step toward him, a crooked smile on my face. "You have nothing to offer the world, Cooper Mackie. You're an oxygen thief, and I don't think it's fair that you continue to exist, quite frankly."

Cooper's eyes widen in understanding, and he licks his lips, the cogs ticking desperately behind his baby blue eyes. "Hey, you can't judge me," he fires back, clearly choosing stupidity over survival. "Only God can do that. You're just a fat bitch! No one wants you— except this fucking jack-O-lantern."

"Ope. You shouldn't have said that. It's obvious that your survival instincts are just as non-existent as you're about to be. Goodbye, Cooper Mackie. I'll probably see you in Hell, sometime." Looking up to Jack, I hold his burning gaze before nodding resolutely.

Cooper turns on his heel and tries to run, but he doesn't get more than a single step before Jack's pumpkin vines lash out like sentient green ropes. They seize his limbs, wrap around his torso, and tighten around his neck, holding him several feet off the ground.

"Do it," I cry, adrenaline pumping through my veins as Jack twists and squeezes while simultaneously ripping outward. Cooper explodes in a spray of bright red beneath the moonlight, the blood misting and showering down upon us as Jack flings Cooper's severed limbs and head into the woods. I laugh and dance in the red rain, running my fingers through my hair, my face upturned toward the stars. "It looks like the wolves won't go hungry, after all!"

A throaty rumble ripples from Jack, and I'm almost certain he's laughing.

Imagine having such a wicked sense of humor after hundreds of years? The thought sets my heart at ease, and suddenly everything feels right with the world. Cooper's days of hurting women are over, and thanks to his very own series of bad choices, he will never procreate, which means one less family of arrogant, conceited, stupid quarterbacks taking up precious real-estate in Farrowville.

Looking down at my blood-stained dress, I bite my lip, a wry smile spreading on my face. "So, Jack, where were we before we were so rudely interrupted?"

My monster seizes me in his tendrils, holding me securely to his chest, and then we're blurring through the night like bleeding shadows, leaving the dark woods in our wake.

Chapter Four

When I open my eyes, we're in an abandoned farmhouse, far across the tangled cornfields and chaff that separates the cultivated land from the wilds. Dust sits like a fine silt upon everything, but it's warmer in here than out in the misty damp of the woods. Jack sets me down on the floorboards, and with his claws, he delicately begins removing my jacket before tearing my stained dress from my body. I feel exposed, standing there in just my boots, lacy bra, and well … not much else.

Jack throws my dress into the fireplace before poking a piece of kindling into his carved eye socket and tossing it in. With the supernatural flames of Hellfire, the hearth is burning merrily in an instant, and my dress—as well as the evidence of Cooper Mackie's glorious demise—burns to cinders. I step closer to the hearth and hold out my hands, allowing the warmth to infuse my flesh and drive away the night's chill.

"Thank you, Jack, for this, and what you did back there. You're my very own Halloween knight."

Jack stares at me with his hollow, blazing eyes and nods.

"I'm glad we understand each other," I say. Turning from him, I lower myself provocatively to the floor and lean back with my knees up, legs spread wide. "Should we get started on that pumpkin patch?"

My monster gets down onto his knees between my legs, his spectacular green cock stiffening before my very eyes. Like magic it begins oozing that delicious candy pre-cum, and I lick my lips at the memory of its taste. I'm almost tempted to rise and clean him up, but

I'm going to need that lubrication down there... Reclining to my elbows on the old floral rug, I bite my lip in anticipation as Jack strokes his head up and down my throbbing slit.

Just feeling his warm monster touch me drives my yearning through the roof, and I reach down with one hand to spread my lips, allowing him easier access. He pushes the head in and I gasp aloud. "Oh, God," I breathe. "You're so fucking huge!"

Jack lowers himself onto his elbows, and his flickering orange gaze finds mine; his trench coat of shadows blocks out all else. There's just us. Me and my ghoulish monster fucking in a derelict farmhouse by a warm Hellfire hearth on All Hallows' Eve. His cock sinks in, slow and steady, one agonizing inch after another. He stretches me like I've never been stretched before. A prolonged moan escapes me, and I adjust my hips as he continues to bury himself inside me.

God, it hurts! Just as badly, if not more than my first time. And then, just when I don't think I can bear to be stretched anymore, his forward momentum stops, and I remember to breathe. I glance down and realize that he's balls deep, all the way in; and I fit him like a fucking glove, albeit an exceptionally tight one. "Oh, Jack," I whisper, reaching up to trail a tentative hand down his smooth pumpkin face. "I'm as ready as I'm ever going to be. Fuck me like the beautifully vicious monster you are. Fill me with your seed like your redemption depends on it."

I don't need to say more. Jack fucks me like a beast, his thick, veined cock plowing my fertile fields with the fury of a jackhammer. The irony is not lost on me. My body vibrates, and I feel like a sock puppet—like something's crawled up inside of me, filling every conceivable part of me—but that only turns me on more.

Vines snake out from under Jack's coat, feeling their way over me, their soft but firm and pliant tendrils finding all the places that drive me nearer to ecstasy.

Tendrils tweak my tender nipples, while delicate, swirling vines find their way between our hot bodies to rub my clit as my monster fucks me into oblivion. Other tendrils slip carefully up my ass, massaging me from behind, before entwining within me to form a twisted, gnarly cock of vines that stretches my ass from the inside, bypassing the uncomfortable ring burn I've experienced with anal sex in the past.

I've never been so thoroughly used and pleasured before! I can hardly stand it. I writhe, sandwiched between Jack and the floor. I want more, and yet, a part of me wants to beg *no more! God, no more!* But I won't beg. I refuse. I found my way to this monster and this moment for a reason, and I will not only withstand whatever pleasures he can draw out of me, but I'll enjoy it. *I'll be strong. Like a vine, I will not break. I'll bend. I'll be pliant, and I'll mold myself into the Woman Who Fucks Monsters.* I am her, and no mere mortal will ever satisfy me again. I know that without a shadow of a doubt. Jack the Trickster has ruined me for all men.

Jack's beautiful green muscular form flexes over me, his supernatural muscles rippling in the dancing shadows of the firelight as he breaks down every wall I have, assaulting every sense I possess. My toes curl, and my thighs clench, my teeth sinking into my lip as I approach the apex of the most intense, soul-destroying orgasm I've ever felt. A scream tears forth from my lips, and I buck like a frantic, broken, desperate animal. Waves of pleasure crash over me, relentless and merciless. I lose feeling in my legs as brutal shudders take hold of me, wracking me from my core, until I'm no longer in control of my own traitorous body.

Incoherent sounds burst out of me as Jack continues to thunder, thrusting like a tireless beast. Then, before I realize what's happening, I find myself flipped over like a bloody pancake, man-handled by his vines so that I now lie prostrate on my belly, my face resting against the old rug. I close my eyes as he re-enters me, and his tendrils adjust position to raise my ass, slipping under once more like sinister fingers to torment my poor, strung-out clit.

On his knees, Jack seizes my hips and just like that, we're going at it doggie style—only I can't hold myself up for the life of me. I have no strength left, and I feel like goo. I don't know where one part of me begins and the next ends. My entire body is slayed by merciless, persistent pleasure. I've never known anything like it. *I don't know that I'm going to survive this! Will I even be able to walk again? It doesn't feel like it.*

The pounding goes on for what seems like an eternity, and I slip into a place of soothing darkness, lulled by Jack's low moans. I feel suspended in time, as if I'm floating. This is what they must mean when they talk about sub-space in BDSM, I realize. When you give yourself over so entirely that the mind takes a backseat and just allows the body to feel, without fear or doubt. You submit to your Dom, giving him complete control and trust.

What am I now? I wonder. *What will I be? The Mother of Monsters? What will I give birth to?* I can't possibly guess. And then a more pertinent thought slithers into my mind, insidious and dark. What will become of Jack? Is he always around, just lurking in the woods, or does he vanish into the ether at the end of All Hallows' Eve? I don't want to be without him. And that's when I know. Amongst our debauchery, and the beautiful spectacle that was the slaughter of Cooper Mackie, I've fallen for Jack the Trickster. *I love my monster.*

As if Jack has heard my thoughts, he growls, and the sound is so thunderous and terrifying that it breaks through the darkness of my mind, slamming me back into my body, back into the present. Jack is thrusting like a demon, his curved claws digging into my flesh as he rides the precipice of his release. Everything is on fire, every nerve, every cell. His tender and cruel tendrils whip my clit, over and over, and the clean sting mixed with the ecstasy that ravages my body pushes me over the edge.

Hands on the floor, my ample breasts wobbling with each violent thrust, I scream until I feel my throat tear. My voice echoes through the abandoned farmhouse as my orgasm pummels me, beating my already brutalized senses like a drum of war. I feel butchered. Absolutely drained. Spent. I have nothing left.

Jack roars, and a part of me is relieved, while the rest of me shrinks at the skin-crawling, horrifying sound that fills the air. It's the song of nightmares breathed into life.

His hot seed pours inside of me as he bucks, and it's an almost comforting feeling in the blissful silence of my mind. The fire in my murdered cunt is extinguished by the massive load of his veined, rock-hard monster cock. And then all I know is fatigue, and a merciful, sweet warmth. It descends upon me like a blanket of peace, prickling through me, melting me, and reducing what remains into a gooey, sticky mess of Halloween honey.

Chapter Five

I roll over and yawn, stretching like a cat. Lazily opening my eyes, I'm greeted by a dim glow—a single candle silently burning in the darkness. I'm in a bed. It smells musty, but at least it's soft. "Jack?" I call out. *He must have carried me here.* I sigh. *Who knew a monster could be so sweet?* "Jack?" I don't know what kind of answer I'm expecting, being that he can't seem to communicate in a traditional sense, but I need to know if he's still here.

Pushing back the covers, I slip from the bed. My boots are still on, and I grin. *Kinky.* Knowing that my dress is nothing but ash, I wander to the old cupboards in the room and open them wide. It smells like mothballs, but there are women's clothes here, and they seem undamaged by time. Grateful, I pull a calf-length white dress down and give it a shake. It's simple, shapeless, and made of cotton, but it will do. Slipping it over my head, I adjust it, then fetch the candle, heading downstairs.

The stairs creak underfoot, giving away my descent. "Jack?" The old house is silent, and a chill manifests at the base of my spine before shivering its way up my back. I shake the feeling away, pursing my lips as I reach the landing. Swallowing the urge to call out again, I wander through the house and find myself back by the hearth. Its flames are bright and fill the room with warmth, which means the fire has been maintained throughout the night; that, or Hellfire doesn't ever burn out…

Panic flutters in my belly. *Where is he? What time is it?* I find my phone on the floral rug, almost lost under the couch. Scooping it up, I swipe the screen and tease my lip through my teeth. It's 4 AM. Pulling on my leather jacket, I slip my phone into my pocket. "Jack?" Opening the front door, I breathe a sigh of relief. He's right there, standing at the front of the house, just beyond the porch. Skipping down the steps, I come to stand beside him.

"Are you all right, Jack?" I ask, glancing up at him.

His fire-filled eyes stare straight ahead.

"Jack?" I move to stand in front of him, but he remains unmoving. His vines are hidden away beneath his black trench coat, and for all intents and purposes he seems just like a very tall, broad-shouldered man with a jack-O-lantern for a head. Unsure of what to do, or what more to say, I take a deep breath, then throw myself at him. Wrapping my arms around him, I rest my head against his green chest. "Please, come back to me," I whisper. "You can't just change my life and go." Strong arms embrace me in return, and I sigh—my fear forgotten.

"Tell me. Show me," I plead, stepping back gently from his arms. "What's wrong?"

Jack rests his clawed hands on my shoulders and leans down, his pumpkin forehead touching mine. Closing my eyes, images flood my mind, and my worst fear surges back, dumping me like a tidal wave. I see Jack in the darkness, alone. It unfolds like hundreds of All Hallows' Eves before. He stands alone, watching as the shadows of night relinquish their hold, and the sun begins to rise, warm and rosy above the horizon. Jack begins to fade from reality, becoming transparent before vanishing in a swirl of black magic in the dawn's light.

I lick my lips and withdraw, a tear rolling down my cheek. "You disappear when Halloween's over," I say, voicing what neither of us wishes to admit. "That's what I thought might happen," I whisper, my lower lip wobbling. "I wish you didn't have to go, Jack."

Jack places a clawed, dark green hand on my belly and meets my gaze. More tears fall. I know exactly what he means to say. He'll be with me in the offspring I carry. "I promise I'll look after them," I say. "I'll birth them here, Jack. This'll be our house. And every Halloween, this is where we'll meet, okay? No need for wolves or dead exes."

My monster inclines his head in agreement, and I smile. "You know, I'm still feeling a little bow-legged, no thanks to you!" I grin, reaching for his hand. "But it's still Halloween as far as I'm concerned, and I could really go for something sweet. What do you say?"

A rumble escapes Jack, and I laugh along with him. If I'm going to have to wait a whole damn year to be loved and fucked by my Halloween beastie, then we're going to make the most of the time we still have!

****

I moan around Jack's cock, delighting in the way his veins throb, pulsing against my tongue. Swirling it around his green head, I draw back to flick his slit, savoring every last drop of candy-sweet pre-cum. Grasping at the middle of his enormous monster with my left, I trail my right down the shaft, all the way to the base, and just like any man, he has a sack. It's firm, and warm, and fills my whole hand. I massage it between my fingers and thumb, rolling them, feeling the testicles within.

My jack-O-lantern growls and runs his claws lightly across my scalp. It sends a shiver through me, titillating my love of risk and danger, and encourages me to deepen my efforts. Slathering his head with saliva, I open wide—as wide as my mouth will go—and take him to the back of my throat, triggering my gag reflex. Jack cradles the back of my head with one large hand, forcing it forward. His hips rock back and forth in a grotesquely seductive fashion as my throat spasms chaotically around him.

I'm in heaven. I've danced in BDSM circles at college, even met some older men who were long-term Dominants, but none of it ever made me feel the way I do right now. The satisfaction of just being used for Jack's pleasure is almost sinful, and it's not long before my ruined cunt is wet and aching, practically begging to be filled and fucked to hell and back, again. My hands tremble and find their way underneath my new dress and between my legs.

A vine seizes my wrist unexpectedly, like a parent slapping their child's hand for reaching for more candy, and I gasp around my mouthful. Glancing up, I swear I can feel the delicious and sinister desire reflected in Jack's permanent, fanged grin. The curling vine returns my hand to the base of his cock before retreating out of sight. A moment later, I moan, grinding myself against the firm vine so eagerly teasing my clit. Warmth fills my heart and soul as I realize just how deeply this monster cares for me. *If I have needs, he will see them met ... aggressively!*

Another vine slithers along my slick flaps, then continues its journey to my ass. I bob my head forward with even more enthusiasm as Jack fucks all my holes at once. *I don't need a man. Not when I have Jack!* Tendrils snake under my dress to wrap around my hard nipples. They alternate between light pinching and twisting, then stroke softly—soothing the tender skin with sweet caresses. *Oh. My. God.* My eyelids flutter closed, and my eyes roll back in my head. *I'm going to cum!* No man has ever done for me what Jack has. The only time I've reached orgasm is when I've done it for myself!

My whole body spasms and vibrates, shaking from within like I've swallowed a bucketful of liquid lightning. I choke on Jack's cock, gasping for air as my release rocks me to my core; and in the next instant, it's running down my thighs to soak the vintage floral rug. As if driven into a frenzy by the scent of my milky musk, my monster fucks my face with the enthusiasm of a crack-addict at a back-alley gloryhole.

Holding my skull in both his enormous hands, he roars as he lets go, his hot, candy-flavored cum filling my throat and mouth. *Dear God. It's too much!* My eyes water with the exertion, but he doesn't relinquish his hold. Riding the waves of his passion to their fullest extent, his seed leaks out my nose and pours from the corners of my mouth. It's like being drowned in cotton candy. *I could think of worse ways to go*, I decide.

Limp and exhausted to my very bones, I finally catch an unhindered lungful of air as Jack pulls out, his cock still dripping and gleaming in the firelight. I sink to my ass in my own wetness. Lifting up the edge of my dress, I wipe my face on the thin cotton and blow the cum out of my head. *And I'm a fucking mess all over again... I'm spending next Halloween utterly naked. Between the two of us, we're a laundromat's worst nightmare!*

Jack sits down in the opposite lounge chair, just watching me.

Licking my lips, I offer him a tired smile. "I think I'm well and truly fucked, Jack. You really have ruined me for all men. You're the only soul I'm ever going to want." My monster curls his fingers, and I crawl across the floor, instinctively climbing into his lap. "I'm going to miss you, my trickster," I whisper against his chest.

The jack-O-lantern pulls his coat of shadows around me like dark wings and holds me close with his monstrous arms, allowing me to soak up his warmth.

"Stay with me," I beseech him as the first rays of morning light shine through the dusty farmhouse curtains. "Just a little while longer." I nestle against him, tucking up my knees and resting my face against his muscular chest—like he's all the protection in the world I'll ever need. The slow, steady beat of his black heart soothes me, like the notes of a sweet lullaby. Fighting fatigue, I feel his sentient vines stroke my hair tenderly, and wipe away my tears. And then, despite my best efforts to cling to consciousness, I fall hopelessly into a deep, dark, and dreamless sleep.

Chapter Six

The sunlight douses me in awareness like an ice-cold bucket of water. My eyes fly open and I find myself alone, curled up on the lounge chair. My monster is gone, and All Hallows' Eve is over. Shivering, despite the warmth of the fire, I hug myself. The evidence of Jack's visit is crisp on my dress, and I bury my face into the white fabric—breathing in the scent of him. Willing his memory to last just a bit longer.

The sense of loss I feel is soul deep, and a hollowness permeates my very being. While the morning chill seems to seep into my veins, chilling my heart and filling me with sorrow. I don't know how long I sit. But I don't want to move. I just want to feel his arms around me. I want him inside me, filling me up so completely that we're no longer two, but one.

And then I remember his seed spewing into my womb, and the feelings of comfort and peace it gave me, and I take heart. Resting my hands on my belly, I close my eyes and speak to the seeds inside me. *Please grow strong. Stay sticky. Don't leave me.*

The next few days are a blur. Cooper's disappearance is all over the local news, and my entire family freaks when I eventually make it back to my parents', disheveled, glassy-eyed, and silent. The police come by to question me, and I tell them the truth—the first part, at least, that he humiliated me and abandoned me at The Lookout. That I tried to walk home through the woods. That I was accosted by wolves, but managed to escape. I tell them I never saw Cooper Mackie again.

Rumors circulate that we were in the woods together, that Cooper came after me and saved me from the wolves at the cost of his own life. A memorial service is held when they find nothing but bones, the town's worst fears confirmed. Everyone assumes he died a hero—protecting me—and that I was so severely traumatized by the horrific incident that I quit college, moving into a nearby farmhouse to see out the rest of my days as a broken recluse.

I did quit college, and I did buy the abandoned farmhouse with my parents' help. But it wasn't because I was traumatized by Cooper Mackie's death. *I'm glad that pig is gone.* But the town's views suit me. They leave me be, and I'm free to spend my time renovating the house, filling it with my art, and nurturing my growing garden.

I never thought I'd settle in Farrowville, to be honest. Never in a million years! I always wanted out of this backwater, hick town, but not anymore. *It's where my heart lives.* And now, I await All Hallows' Eve like an eager child ready to hit the streets trick-or-treating...

****

The moon rises and a thrill races through me, starting at my toes and fizzling out at my cold nipples. I bite my lip in nervous excitement as I trail my gaze over my well-tended pumpkin patch. My half-dozen pumpkins are my pride and joy. I've watched them grow from the size of my fist into shining orange globes that could take prizes at the town fair. They're my babies, and tonight, when the moon reaches its zenith, they'll awaken—and Jack's legacy will be born.

As naked as the day I came into this world, I sit beneath the stars, eyes closed, sitting cross-legged on a blanket by the pumpkin patch. I'm feeling chilly, but it doesn't matter. My body will soon thrum with warmth. *He's going to come back for me.* I know it in my bones. You don't connect, and fuck like that, and not come back. *No amount of Halloween haunting could keep him away.*

I'm sure of it.

Just as the brilliance of the moon bathes the farm in its glory, I feel a gentle tendril stroke my cheek. My eyes are open before I draw my next breath, and I leap from the blanket, spinning on my heel toward the cornfields. And there he is, silhouetted by the moonlight, dark, sinister, and just as big as I remember. The Hellfire burns bright behind his carved eyes, and my heart sings.

"Jack!" I cry, throwing myself at him.

He catches me with his many vines and draws me into his chest, wrapping his arms around me.

"You're back," I whisper. "I knew you'd come!" I wiggle against him, and he lowers me to the rich earth. "And you're just in time. The babies will awaken, tonight, right? I've looked after them, just like I promised I would."

Jack follows me to the pumpkin patch and gazes down on what we created together. I think he's proud. I feel the warmth emanating from him, even a foot away.

We stand together, side by side, and I grasp for his clawed hand as the soil of the patch starts to fuss. First, one pumpkin—then another—begins to move, jiggling in the ground. Vines reach out, and our first baby jack-O-lantern is born, crawling from the rich, moist earth. It toddles about, all willy-nilly, directionless and confused.

Jack stoops down and picks up his child, holding it carefully in the crook of one arm before bringing a clawed finger to its orange flesh. I gasp as he sinks his sharp claw in, carving out eyes, a nose, and finally a mouth. Then, holding the baby aloft, he rests his forehead to the baby's and breathes his fire into it, lighting up its menacing little features with a tiny, blazing Hellflame of its very own.

"Oh my God," I whisper, as he passes the infant

to me. I clutch the little one to my chest, and a tear escapes my eye. "He's just beautiful!" The other five follow, and soon our little army of Lanterns are toddling about, tearing through the garden and terrorizing one another in picture-perfect Halloween fashion. "We did it, Jack," I say, as we watch them play. "You have your legacy, and a family of your own." I sigh, my heart swelling with a monster mother's love. "But what now?"

The jack-O-lantern scoops me off my feet, throws me over his shoulder, and swooshes us into the house in a swirl of shadow. Wasting no time, he rips open his black trench coat. I bite my lip at the gleaming, hard green cock that awaits me. Its familiar veins pulse, and I can already smell his sweetness.

"So, this is it, then? From now on, we spend some time with the kids, and then fuck like mad rabbits every Halloween?" My monster lover rumbles with mirth, and I grin in response. "Well, okay, then. That's fine by me. Trick-or-treating is over-rated if you ask me!"

Sinking to my knees, I take his cock in hand and languorously lick the tip. Jack's candy-flavored pre-cum is just like I remember—sickeningly sweet, but so moreish that you could never have your fill! Lapping it all up, he continues to ooze, and I glance up, raising an intrigued brow. "I think I have a better idea," I say. Then, taking Jack's hand, I lead him to the dining table. Tossing him a cheeky wink, I hop up, scooching back on my ass. *Foregoing clothes this Halloween was the best idea!* Lying down, I spread my legs, beckoning Jack with a curling finger. "I've missed you, and I know you've missed me."

Jack approaches the table, his eyes blazing with lust. He strokes his enormous cock with one clawed hand, milking the pre-cum onto my already glistening, wet slit. Then, rubbing the bulbous head up and down, he spreads the candy-sweet lubricant, priming me for entry.

I feel that familiar, delicious pressure as he eases his beast into position, and I whimper in desperate anticipation and need. "Drive it home, Jack," I beg.

And he does. As his firm balls slap my ass, I howl, my poor hole stretching for dear life to once more accommodate my monster. Grabbing my legs, he hooks my knees over his shoulders and pounds me like he hasn't seen me for three-hundred and sixty-four days.

My groans of pain soon become moans of ecstasy as he plunders the deepest parts of me. Panting, with a mischievous grin on my face, I give myself over to the monster—submitting, mind, body, and soul.

My thoughts stray as Jack ravages me, wandering back to that unforgettable night in the woods on All Hallows' Eve one year ago... Following my deviant little heart and giving in to my debauched and sinister Halloween desires was definitely the best decision I've ever made. And I'd make it again.

The End

FAEDRA ROSE

DEATHLY DESIRES

Loving Monsters, 2

Faedra Rose

Copyright © 2023

Chapter One

They say the veil between the worlds is thin tonight, no more than a gossamer whisper between the seen and unseen. Halloween has always been my favorite holiday. I've decided, fittingly, that this one will be my last. I can't handle living anymore—it's just too painful.

Glancing down at my scarred wrists, I pull my long black sleeves down further to hide my shame and heave a sigh. It's strange how some people lead such wonderful lives, while the rest of us endure such wretched ones. *We aren't living. Not really.* Most of us are barely surviving. Hell, we're hanging on grimly by bloody fingernails, just trying to make ends meet.

I didn't ask to be born into an abusive, drug-riddled household. I didn't ask for a childhood of cigarette burns and purple bruises. I didn't ask to be violated again and again by Mom's one thousand different junkie boyfriends. I didn't ask to be the only real adult. I don't fucking like working two shitty jobs just to pay our rent and keep something other than alcohol and rollie papers in the fucking pantry because my own mother is a useless addict. *But here I am.*

My mom's never protected me from the monsters in her life, so they bled easily into mine, like shadows through the cracks of our broken lives. From what I've heard, her formative years mirror my own. Ever since I can remember, she's been lost. Lost in her own wonderland, or nightmare, forever escaping life and its demons, while never leaving it. She's afraid. I know that much. She has the courage to face the pointy end of a needle, or another filthy fist, but she hasn't the courage to change it or leave it all behind. She can't. *Or won't.*

I see the resignation in her eyes every single day, and every single day it crushes my soul a little more. She's resigned herself to a living death—night after night of blurring the edges of her reality—just trying to forget what she feels. All I know is that's not going to be me. *I'm more afraid of not living than dying.* Death is the answer to all my problems. It's my cure. It's the real escape from it all. There's no half-assing it. Once I commit, it'll be done ... and hopefully I'll finally find peace.

There's no surviving a fall like this. I'll either be smashed on the submerged rocks, or, if I manage to miss them, the impact of the water alone will be like landing on solid ground, and I'll break my back. My ribs will likely puncture my lungs, and I'll drown in a mix of my own blood and the dark waters of the lake. It's comforting, if I'm being honest. I can't endure my present situation any longer, and if I were to survive my suicide attempt and be left in a vegetative state? A shudder runs through my bones as the cool night air whispers over me, whipping up my lank, rainbow-dyed hair. I need the guarantee of death, because no one in this damn world is going to look after me, and no one is going to bloody miss me, anyway.

That's the cruelty of a disadvantaged life. *I'm at the bottom of the food chain.* No one except junkies want to know me. And even then, they only want to associate for the occasional no-strings-attached fuck, or for the chance to score their next hit at a discounted price. Even if I wanted to better myself, and my life, there's little to no hope of a brighter future. They say there is, the jerks on high who think they speak for the people, but there isn't.

I'm an abused nineteen-year-old from the backwaters of Green Pines in Washington State. It's not even so much a county in its own right as it is a ramshackle trailer park growing on the edge of the forest along the banks of Black Lake. Like a cancer, or a fungus, it just seems to grow, expanding as more trash blows in. There's a gas station up on the highway, and not much else. I have to catch the bus to work in the next town over because I can't afford a car, and then I end up walking back, alone—after my shifts—in the dead of night.

It's fucked. All of it. And I've had enough! I've had enough of looking after my useless mother, providing for us, and being the touch toy of every stinking creep in the area. *I'm done! I'm really fucking done.* I'm going to jump, fly for a few seconds, and then that'll be all she wrote. I'll be free.

I chug the last of my beer and leave the bottle on the rocks. A sort-of monument to my demise. Standing, I brush off my skirt and rake my fingers through my hair, casting my gaze over the edge of the rocky ledge. The dark waters call to me from below, like sirens at sea, with the promise of eternal peace.

Sucking in a lungful of brisk, fall air, I grimace. "This is it," I say. "Happy Halloween, Green Pines. It's been shitty knowing you." Turning, I get a run up. It just feels like the thing to do. To go out in an epic fashion, rather than simply and anticlimactically stepping off the cliff. Heart racing, I pump my arms, covering the distance from the shadowed tree-line to the edge in seconds—and then I'm committed.

I'm falling, my rainbow hair streaming above me as the dark, moonlit reflective waters of Black Lake draw near. The stars shimmer above, and swirling mist floats along the distant shore. It's beautiful. All logic screams at me to brace for impact, to prepare for the pain, but I don't. I just fall, closing my eyes as the frigid water steals the breath from my lungs, and pain radiates through me. I feel the icy embrace of the lake wrapping me up like a lover, and I sink into the darkness. Everything is a blur of pain and cold, but I can almost taste peace. It's just a breath away.

The air bubbles from my mouth and nostrils as I descend into the depths. It's so quiet and serene. I watch as they wobble up toward the moonlit surface, and a smile tugs at the corners of my lips. *I made the right choice.* Just as I close my eyes again to commit to my final sleep, a vise-like grip seizes my wrist, and a shadowed, skeletal form swims into my vision. Hollow, dark sockets stare into my soul, and I scream—the last of my breath escaping in a rush of bubbles as oblivion claims me.

Chapter Two

Opening my eyes, I feel a burning pressure in my lungs. Rolling over, I instinctively purge the cold water onto the misty shore. *The misty shore?* Eyes wide, frozen from head to toe, I glance around, solid earth beneath me once more. Black Lake glitters and the moon is full and familiar, but something is undeniably different. Something feels off, though I can't quite put my finger on it...

How am I alive? How did I make it to the shore? I have questions but no answers. *Did someone save me? Why can't I feel any pain?* Raising myself to a seated position, I shiver, rubbing my arms vigorously for warmth. "Hello?" I call out, looking left, then right. "Is anyone here?" In the distance, I see something floating in the water, but it's hard to make out, so I refocus my attention to my present situation. "Hello?" I call again. This time, cold slides up my spine like jagged ice crystals sprouting beneath my skin.

I feel fear. It arrests me, paralyzing me for several breathless moments. Every baser instinct within me screams *Run!* Something dangerous lingers just behind me, hidden within the shadows of the forest. I can't explain how I know it. I just do. And then the soul-chilling vision in the lake comes back to me, and I grasp my wrist in recollection. My lower lip trembles as I remember the hollow, dark, and seemingly endless gaze of the spectral figure that seized me as I sank toward my peace.

The paralysis passes and I can move. Slowly, so agonizingly slowly, I turn toward the forest behind me. My breath hitches in my throat as a billowing black cloak comes into view. Swallowing my fear, I force myself to look up. The figure stands at least seven feet tall, towering over me with the authority of death itself. In its grip it holds a sinisterly sharp scythe; it's long, cruel, curved blade glints in the moonlight. And then there's that face—or the lack thereof. It stares back at me, no more than a literal cowled skull, the promise of a dark eternity lurking within its empty sockets.

"Holy shit," I breathe.

The spectral figure tilts its expressionless head, bony fingers clinking one after the other against the gnarled and ancient-looking wood of its terrifying weapon.

"Oh my God." The realization hits me like a blow to the stomach, and I gasp as my final moments play out in my mind again. "I'm dead," I whisper. Warm tears spring from my eyes, betraying some inner sense of hope I never knew I possessed. "You're the Grim Reaper, and you're here to claim my soul, aren't you?" I swallow the deep, dark dread that lingers in the pit of my stomach. I nod, more to myself than the reaper as my suspicions are confirmed. "This is what I wanted and I got it."

A million thoughts rush through my mind like a bullet train wobbling at high speed on its rails. *Was I wrong to end it? Did I cut my potential short? Could I have escaped my reality and forged a new path ... somehow? Does any of it even matter anymore?* I'm dead and presumably on the other side of the veil, no longer in the realm of the physical.

Rising to my feet solemnly, weighted by the heaviness of my choice, I adjust my sodden sweater and straighten my skirt. "Okay," I say, swallowing my fear. "I'm ready."

The reaper stares back at me, seemingly uncomprehending.

I lick my lips and shuffle my feet on the pebbled shore. "I'm ready to pass over, or disappear, or whatever happens when you die…"

The reaper shakes its skull head slowly then and drops its scythe to the ground, the sound jarring in the silent landscape.

The action surprises me, and I step back, uncertain. "W—what are you doing?"

The reaper grins, opening its skeleton maw as it shrugs off its shadowy cowl.

I imagine my jaw hitting the damp earth beneath my feet as the black cloak falls soundlessly, revealing a partially tangible body of shadow. It's solid and not. It's transparent where the darkness thins, and I can see his bone-white skeleton underneath.

Squinting my eyes in the moonlight, I can determine the semblance of a face, and hands, features that betray a darkly handsome entity. *What the fuck?* The reaper is ripped as fuck. The swirling darkness of his form reveals abs that look mouth-wateringly chiseled. Like a ladder for curious fingers, they lead down to a smooth V, and to a horrifyingly huge shadow cock. How tangible his form appears to the eye seems to depend on the light.

I'm lost for words as he spreads his arms wide before curling a long, shadowy, and bony finger.

Did the Grim Reaper just flash me right now? And did he really just drop his robe and come hither me? I want to say I don't know what this specter of death could want of me, but I'm not stupid, and I wasn't born yesterday. The Grim Reaper wants me to suck his fucking shadow meat! "Holy shit." I step closer, my feet acting of their own accord. "Is this the way I pay my toll? Like my silver coin to the Ferryman?" I ask, my gaze trained firmly on the pulsing, hard cock between us. "No cock, no afterlife? Is that it?" An insane laugh escapes me, the absurdity of my situation momentarily overcoming my fear. "Wow! I wish I could just hang out with you and see how all the God-botherers react when they die! I'd pay to see their faces."

A dark rumble that sounds suspiciously like laughter fills the brisk air.

"Oh, good. Death has a sense of humor." The reaper strokes his cock and a shiver runs through me. "So, if I do this, I'll find peace, right?" I press. "I guess reaping souls is a pretty lonely job. No down time? Okay. Why not? Sure. I'll blow you, and then I'm paid up? That seems fair, I suppose." *Honestly, I've had far more revolting and sickening sods touch me and force me into submission in life.* And truthfully? I'd be lying if I didn't admit that some dark, fucked-up part of me finds this not only immensely terrifying and amusing, but a bullshit huge fucking turn-on.

The reaper seems to read my mind and, placing his hands on my head, gently pushes me down, guiding me to kneel. "So, you can't talk, huh?" I ask. "That's cool. Talking's overrated anyway." Using my knees to adjust the earth to my comfort, I turn my gaze to the pulsating, throbbing shadow cock mere inches from my face. *Seems fitting that it should end like this for me...*

Chapter Three

Reaching out a cautious hand, I tentatively touch the shifting shadows with my fingertips. A gasp escapes me, and I withdraw my hand in shock. It might appear intangible, but that cock is definitely solid and hard as a rock. I glance up at the reaper, lick my lips, and then reach out again, this time a little more confidently. The reaper groans—the sound no more than a rasping whisper—as I trail my cool fingers up and down his brutally impressive length. *He must be nearly ten inches? ... Jesus! I wonder what it—I mean, what he tastes like? The grave? Ice?*

Filled with equal amounts of nerve-wracking anticipation and prickly dread, I languidly drag my tongue around his head. It's smooth and surprisingly warm, and as cold as I am it feels like Heaven—like a long, thick hand warmer endowed with visibly throbbing veins. A shiver runs up my spine, and I become suddenly aware that my nipples feel as cold as icicles. They strain against the sodden fabric of my black sweater, desperately tender and chilled.

Spurred on by my body's illicit reaction to the sight and feel of the reaper's monstrous cock, I take his slick head into my mouth. Wrapping my lips around its base, I begin to suck. My eyes grow wide and I gasp around the appendage in my mouth. *What the fuck?* Holding his shaft, I draw back, flicking my tongue along the slit of his dark beast. *I must be going fucking insane!* Dead and insane? I suppose anything's possible. The reaper's pre-cum tastes like melted chocolate—like, legitimately. Not chocolate-flavored syrup, but rich, pure, real creamy liquid chocolate! It's my favorite treat. I love chocolate everything! It's my one weakness. My very own addiction! *How in the Hell...?*

Maybe blowing the Grim Reaper for eternity wouldn't be such a bad thing? I mean, my reaper's totally hot in this shit-your-pants, have-a-heart-attack, abuse-me-now-Sir kind of way; and the fucker tastes like freaking chocolate! *Count me in. Who needs eternal peace when you can have sex and chocolate? I mean, really?* Settling into a comfortable position, I set to work. I don't know how often Mr. Grim gets his rocks off, but I'm going to blow this guy like, well, my eternal life depends on it.

Licking up and down his shaft, I delight in the feel of his veins against my tongue. For someone so apparently dead-like, he feels very alive and full of life, or at least something like it. My reaper combs his long, skeletal fingers through my wet rainbow locks, and I shiver as I feel sharpness—like curved claws against my scalp. Opening my mouth wide, I take Mr. Grim to the back of my throat, moaning around his cock as his grip on my hair tightens, causing little trails of lightning to sting and dance across my skin.

My reaper is a bit of a sadist it seems. And for the first time in my life—or *unlife*—the thought drives me wild and gets me wet like crazy. Almost every time I've been dominated has been against my will, with guys I was repulsed by. This is something else entirely. The Grim Reaper terrifies me on some level, but I'm also inexplicably drawn to him. His domination is subtle and allows me to choose my level of control. And I get the feeling he wants me just as much if not even more than I want him. *The Grim Reaper wants me? Hot.*

The reaper groans as I hold his shadowy cock in my spasming throat. Suppressing my gag reflex, I wriggle forward until my hands can trace the length of his cock and trail over that sexy-as-fuck V and around his hips to his ass. I cling to his muscular backside, digging into the shadowed flesh with my black-lacquered nails.

The reaper growls. I glance up—mouth full of monster cock—to meet his hollow gaze, only to notice pinpoints of sentient black fire burning within. He grins then, and against his bare-toothed grin I see the semblance of dark lips curling into a vicious smile.

I moan as he tightens his fingers in my hair and forcefully draws my head back, giving me barely a second to gasp for air before he thrusts, slamming my head forward to fuck my throat with deliciously cruel abandon. All I can do is endure it. I focus on keeping my throat relaxed, my mouth wide, and my lips firm as I cut into his ass even deeper in a mimicry of protest. *You like to play rough, fucker?* Two can play at that game.

Underneath my skull-and-crossbones mini-skirt, Mr. Grim has me dripping warmth down the inside of my cold thighs. My insides begin to ache and my poor clit throbs, desperate for attention. I can't remember the last time I was horny and felt good about it. To be honest, I can't remember the last time I actually fucking wanted it. The ball's never been in my court, but now it is, and I do want it. God damn, I want to be claimed by the Grim Reaper! And if all I am now is a soul, then I want him to fuck my bloody soul! My need to feel that rigid, veined shadow cock deep inside me is madness inducing.

Lost in my own desire, I'm suddenly snapped back to the moment by a searing burn across my scalp, and the sensation of thick, hot, chocolate-flavored cum oozing down my throat. I gag, but he holds me tight. I swallow as best as I'm able around his immense girth. *Fucking Hell, it's delicious. But I might bloody well drown in it!*

"Mm," I moan as he pulls back, rubbing his gleaming head around my lips like sweet, sticky lipstick.

I lick the heavenly goo from my lips, using my finger to wipe around the corners of my mouth before sucking it clean, my gaze fixed firmly upon Mr. Grim's.

Something in my look must trigger the darkness within, because in the next second the reaper seizes me by my hair and drags me from the shore to the edge of the moonlit forest. He roughly tosses me over a large, damp, fallen tree, and I cry out as I hit the wet bark, momentarily winded. It's only then that I realize what's about to happen, and my world view narrows to my wet-ass pussy as Mr. Grim tears my black panties from me as easily as if they were made of tissue paper—leaving my bare ass and my glistening cunt exposed to the cool whisper of the All Hallows' Eve breeze.

Chapter Four

"Wait! Oh my God." I gasp, trying to look backward, but the reaper holds me down, a large, firm hand placed between my shoulder blades. His strength and desire to dominate me has me dripping, and I whimper in frustration and wanting. *But he has such a huge cock! Bigger than I've ever taken before! What if he rips me open?* I'm confounding myself. It's insanity! With one breath I want that big, fat cock ramming me over the tree, and with the next fear bubbles like a spring beneath the surface.

Wait. What am I freaking out about? What is there to fear? *It's not like he can fuck me to death. I can't die twice. I'm already dead!* Licking my lips in anticipation, I push my ass up, cheekily wiggling it from side to side. "Come on then. Fuck me like you mean it!"

The reaper presses his hand down harder, forcing my face to the damp wood—effectively commanding my silence—and I can all but feel my pussy quiver with hunger. His large, smooth head slides up and down my sopping wet cunt lips, and it takes all my willpower not to push back. I can't explain it, but I've never wanted someone so badly! I whimper like a mewling kitten. "Please, Sir," I beg. "I need you, Mr. Grim."

The reaper smacks my ass, then sinks his vein-rippled, shadow cock inside me, all the way to the hilt. His dark sac slaps against me, and I cry out in ecstasy. My pulsating insides clutch at him, desperate to keep him, but he withdraws all the way, taunting and teasing me with his head—dipping it *just* into my slick wetness before pulling back.

"You're a fucking monster," I sulk as my

fingernails find purchase on the damp bark.

Mr. Grim seems amused by my need. He slides inside my warm, moist pussy with deep, long, slow strokes.

And I hate it. *Fucking God, I hate it!* It's agonizing. I can't take it. It's murderous and cruel. He's purposely denying me and taking his sweet time. But I want him to fuck me like a wild thing. I want to feel his great cock sawing me in fucking half. *This slow bullshit is torture! Torture!* I squirm beneath him, becoming increasingly frustrated. "Is this my punishment?" I ask. "Did I do something wrong?" When he stops suddenly inside me, but continues to grind his hips against me, I break. I can't. I just fucking can't. *I'm not above begging. I need that cock to ravage me more than I've ever needed anything.*

"Please!" I sob, unexpected tears spilling down my cheeks. "Fuck my cunt, hard, please! I need it. I'll do anything for it. You can even bury that huge cock in my ass if you want to, afterwards! Please! Just. Fill. Me."

Seemingly intrigued by my offer or perhaps striking upon some semblance of empathy, the reaper drags his fingers down my spine, his claws tinglingly like fire over my cool flesh. And I know I've won. Surely. *No guy in the universe ever says no to ass. And I don't think the Grim Reaper will be the first to turn it down.*

Before I can process another thought, the reaper seizes my hips, his claws piercing my skin as he ensures a brutal and steadfast grip. I shriek with shock. I can feel his fucking claws physically in me. I can feel the snare of them curling into my flesh—but it doesn't hurt. At least, not the way I expected it to, and it's an utter head-fuck. But it doesn't matter. None of it does, because Mr. Grim is merciful and does just as I asked. He sinks his cock deep inside with an unfathomable and unnatural speed, and God does it feel incredible! I can hear my cunt squelching as he rails me, and I forget how to breathe ... or even if I need to.

Throwing my head back, I rest on my forearms, keening and panting like a wounded animal. And for the first time I understand it. The desire of men to use women. To fuck them like meat and claim them as trophies. How exquisite it must be to have such power! To use your cock like a weapon and hear the cries of ecstasy and anguish it causes. To reduce a woman with dreams, and wants, hopes and desires, to a screeching, desperate fuck toy that craves your cock more than air. No man has ever made me feel this way before. And the reaper is no man. Just as well I'm dead, because after this I could never go back. The fucking Grim Reaper has ruined me for all men!

My breasts bounce against the fallen tree, and incomprehensible sounds spill from my lips. I can't stay quiet. Or maybe I just don't want to. It's so freeing to fuck noisily and unapologetically. My sex has almost always been about abuse. It's been secret and threatening, hidden behind thin trailer park doors and loud music, fueled by drugs and alcohol. I had to be as silent as a mouse—I was even gagged, and had a gun held to my head, once.

But this is not like that. *This is everything I want.* There are no threats here. Just unparalleled amounts of pleasure. I'm already gone anyway, lost to the other side of the veil. There's just me and my sopping wet cunt, my grunting mouth, my tight, puckering asshole—and death. If this is the only time I ever get to experience such perfect, wild abandon, then I will milk it for every damn second that I have.

Fear fills me so immediately and so suddenly that I'm dragged back to the present, slammed back into the now from the delicious, mindless zone Mr. Grim's jackhammering between my thighs had transported me to. *I can't feel my legs.* I can't feel anything in fact. It's like I'm suspended between a breathless pause and a gleaming knife's edge. Then I'm gasping and sobbing as a towering tidal wave of pure, hot, knee-weakening ecstasy crashes down on me.

It pushes me under and I tumble through the black, starless eternity of myself like a rag doll drowning in bliss. A second wave of heat explodes within me, and the world falls away until there's nothing left but fire within, chewing me up from the inside like a ravenous beast. My wordless scream fills the void of the hereafter, echoing through the veil.

I'm at the mercy of the reaper, and I have never come so hard. And I think it's far from over.

Chapter Five

I flop against the fallen tree, exhausted, as my body spasms with the aftershocks of my multiple orgasm. *That was intense.* How can I possibly survive more? *Has anyone else been fucked by the reaper?* I wonder. *Am I really the first? Or am I just another broken woman in a long line of wretched souls and suicides?* "Mr. Grim?" I breathe.

The reaper smacks my ass again and withdraws with a sloppy *pop!* jerking his hot, sweet load all over my pretty pink starfish. I squirm as one long finger traces my asshole, leisurely coaxing his chocolate cum inside me … prepping me for anal.

"Can you," I hesitate, unsure of my own voice, but certain of what I want. "Can you tie me up? I—I kind of like it. It makes me feel safe."

The Grim Reaper growls and I shiver. It's a deep, lust-filled, and fright-inducing sound that only serves to turn me on even more. The next thing I know, I'm bodily lifted from the log and thrown over the reaper's shoulder as if I were light as a feather. I shriek in delight and surprise. My supernatural host's muscles flex beneath me, and I long to run my hands over them.

In the blink of an eye, I'm upright and fastened to an enormous pine tree. Gasping, I tilt my head back, craning my neck to watch in awe as wisps of shadow snake around my wrists and around the trunk. The reaper kicks my feet out, spreading my legs wide, and more bonds of shadow wrap each ankle, meeting each other around the tree to secure me in position. With my legs open and my arms above my head, I feel defenseless and helpless, yet somehow the bindings offer me comfort.

And I eat up every damn moment of it.

Mr. Grim lowers his shadow-fleshed skull face to mine and drags his long, hot, black forked tongue up my cheek. It's so erotic I could almost cry in pathetic, desperate need.

I hold his gaze, challenging him. "I might be in a vulnerable state, but I'm not afraid," I warn. "Do your worst. I can take it. I want it."

The reaper grins in his deeply perturbing way, then trails his claws down my body, cutting my sweater to ribbons in the process. He tweaks my hard nipples between his shadow fingers, and I gasp at the exquisite pain amplified by the cold. Then, grasping my breasts, one in each hand, he licks and sucks, my flesh disappearing in and out of view within his semi-transparent maw.

"Oh God," I moan, struggling against my bonds, both yearning for and wanting to escape the deliciously sinful ministrations of his unnaturally long tongue. And then he does something no man has ever done for me. I've been subjected to most things, including flashlights and deodorant cans... I've been fingered and fucked, but no man has ever pleasured me with his own mouth before.

The reaper sinks to his knees and spreads my whisker with his fingers, that long tongue of his flicking out to lick at my clit, tasting the way a serpent scents the air.

"Fuck." I wasn't expecting it to feel so alive and so damn sensitive. The ham-fisted finger fumbling I've been forced to endure in the past made my clit raw and sore. I can only assume the fucked-up morons had no idea what they were doing, or how to please a woman. *Those selfish fucking perverts!* I fume in between gasps. *But not Mr. Grim.* He's treating me the way a woman ought to be treated. With passion and desire and a yearning to see me fulfilled as much as himself.

The reaper laps at my slit—hungry for my cream—before his tongue snakes inside me.

I moan, feeling the warmth of his curious tongue flexing and darting, longer even than I gave it credit for. It's beastly, and feels so monstrously wrong that it's perfectly right. I writhe against the tree, grinding my cunt against his grotesquely beautiful skull face. *But I couldn't care less about how he looks. I just want to feel good!* I was as alternative in life as I am in death, and I'd be lying if I didn't admit that the Grim Reaper is genuinely alluring in his own spooky and surreal, otherworldly kind of way.

My pleasure builds to intolerable levels. I bite my lip hard enough to draw blood, but the reaper brutishly hastens his devilry, his attentions relentless and maddening. "Fuck me," I whine. It seems terribly unfair that he can make me feel so damn cock-hungry! I've never wanted to be claimed so completely and brutally in my life. Violence has always felt like an invasion. But now it's forbidden ecstasy—a whispered secret known only to those few who truly belong in darkness.

Lost in the sensations wracking my body, my mind turns to mush as Mr. Grim forces me to experience the most shockingly intense orgasm of my life. It's single-handedly *more* in every conceivable way than the multiple orgasm I enjoyed just minutes ago. I literally lose all feeling in my legs, and I sag against my bonds, my clit on fire. It's so fucking painful that I see stars and shadows dance as I buck and thrash like a pitiful, dying fish on the sand.

My lips part to scream, but no sound escapes them. The silence of my climax is deafening, and still the reaper works, sinfully dragging out each exquisite drop of brutal pleasure for the sheer fun of seeing me suffer on the edge of Heaven and Hell.

Hot tears spill, and I give up control completely, no longer able to withstand the torment assaulting me. Broken, spent, with no strength left to sustain me, I hang from the tree, a rainbow-haired, spoiled dolly—a toy well-used. *If this is what death is like, kill me a thousand times over!* Sticky, light-headed, and jelly-legged, I feel my grip on reality fading as a sweet and heavy blanket of fatigue drapes over me.

The reaper releases me then. Scooping me up in his arms, he cradles me close to his transparent shadow flesh, keeping me warm beneath his billowing black cloak. Not giving a damn about whether I ever open my eyes again, I close them with a smile on my face as he settles down with me by the shore. *This is the love I always deserved* is the last conscious thought I manage before darkness claims me.

Chapter Six

The world takes on a strange, hazy, and surreal quality. *Am I dreaming?* We're no longer snuggled by the lake... We're somewhere else, somewhere cosmically black and star-spangled. I just don't know where. *How many layers of reality are there?* It's like we're in-between universes. My mind boggles. "Mr. Grim?" I call out into the endless, shifting mist. A gentle hand comes to rest on my shoulder. I glance back, relief flooding me. *It's him.* "Where are we?" I ask.

The reaper points ahead with his free hand. Light pierces through the darkness, and a swirling circular portal appears before us. I shield my eyes against the brightness, until they adjust, then squint ahead, a gasp escaping me. Another world manifests within the portal. A single word slips unbidden from my lips like a reverent prayer. "Beautiful." I don't need an explanation to understand what I'm looking at.

Endless green hills stretch from horizon to horizon. Glittering waterfalls spill into crystal-clear lakes, and flowers of every color known to man bloom from the verdant earth, breathtaking in their splendor. The sky is cloudless and goes on forever, eternally blue. I see people—other souls—all in their prime, enjoying the majestic paradise before my eyes. They run and dance, the sound of song and laughter ringing clear. Others sit together in pairs and family groups, reliving memories, lost in their own dreams of happiness and peace.

"Heaven," I breathe. I catch the reaper nodding out of the corner of my eye. Licking my lips, I take an involuntary step forward. "Is this real? Can I go there?" I ask. "Is this where I belong?"

Mr. Grim squeezes my shoulder in response.

"I don't know why, but I never really believed, let alone thought I'd be worthy of Heaven," I say. "I've been defiled and used, done drugs, drunk myself into oblivion, and stolen from others. I've even cursed my mom for giving me life." I flinch at the painful memory. "I remember telling her that she was a fucking failure, and that I wish she'd had the guts to abort me." I stare blankly ahead, watching as the souls of Heaven enjoy their reward for lives well lived, oblivious to my presence lingering just on the outskirts of their world.

"If I go, I'll never see you again, will I?" I ask, turning to look up into his dark hood.

The reaper shakes his head, and a tangible cold emanates from him.

Sadness, I realize with a tug on my heart. "And still, you'd show me the way? You'd let me go? Even though what we have is…" I pause, considering my words. "It's unlike anything I've ever known. To me, being with you feels like Heaven." I gesture toward the shimmering portal. "And this place? It doesn't seem like the kind of place I want to be. Prettiness forever? And who will I have to share it with? The loved ones I've never had? Random souls? Like making friends in kindergarten all over again?" I shake my head and bite my lower lip. "I don't think so. That's not on the cards for me—not if I have a say, Sir."

I take the reaper's skeletal hand in mine, interlacing our fingers. "Can't I stay with you? In-between life and death? I know you feel alone, but maybe you don't have to? Maybe it doesn't have to be that way? We could be weirdos … together." I smile.

The reaper taps his scythe, and the portal wobbles, blurring and warping until a new scene is revealed. There is no mistaking the nightmare that is Hell. Fiery mountains burn, while rivers of blood run through a cracked and toxic landscape. The screams of the damned are deafening, and I feel nauseous as the despair and dread tangibly leaks through the portal. *This is not where I want to end up.* But it's what my fucking abusers deserve ... an eternity of pain and anguish, to know the fear and despair I've felt all these years.

And that's when the most brilliant thought occurs to me, like a lightbulb switching on above my head. "What if I could help you do your job?" I ask. "There's God in Heaven, and the Devil in Hell, right? They have countless souls and servants—angels and demons— carrying out their bidding eternally. But who helps you? You're the Angel of Death! It's a heavy burden to bear. Reaping the souls of the dead and ferrying them to the Afterlife is an almighty task, and you shouldn't have to serve that purpose alone. So, what if you keep me in this limbo with you? I could become a spirit of justice, and whisper into the ears of the sick fucks of the world to end themselves! We can save the innocent from real predators, like a cosmic clean-up crew, or something, purging the Earth of its rotten fruit."

The reaper remains still for a time, seemingly contemplating my proposition.

"Come on, Mr. Grim," I purr, trailing a teasing hand over his abs and further beneath his robe. "You're an archangel! You deserve this small pleasure. The angels in Heaven get their paradise, and the fallen get their debauchery and chaos. You deserve my company. You deserve *us*. We obviously happened for a reason. Besides, isn't God omniscient? Isn't everything supposedly his Divine will? If that's truly the case, then everything that has ever happened to me happened for a reason. It made me who I am and it brought us to this very moment! I haven't been sucked into Heaven, or smote to Hell … which can only mean that what I'm saying right now is meant to be. You chose me because we are meant to be together. Don't you see?"

The Grim Reaper wraps his arms around me, holding me close. With my ear against his shadowed chest, I can hear the strange rhythm of his supernatural heart and find it offers me great comfort. I never want to be apart from it.

"You know what?" I say defiantly. "It's happening. You can't make me go through either portal, and I'm pretty sure what I spotted floating back there in the lake was my dead ass corpse. So, I'm done. I'm in-between life and death, and it's bloody well where I'm going to stay—with you."

Chapter Seven

The reaper's skull face grins, and in this strange place between all things, I see his shadow flesh far more clearly. Beneath his deathly façade he's angelically beautiful, erotically and skin-chillingly so. Then, for the first time, he reveals his immense obsidian black feathered wings—all six of them. They spread behind him, majestic as fuck, leaving me breathless and in awe. I'd expect nothing less of the Angel of Death.

Trailing his hand over my face, his clawed fingers gently coax my eyelids to close. A moment later I feel his hand resting over my heart, and then an incomprehensible pain tears through me, exploding from my heart. It sears through my fragile veins like fire. I open my mouth to scream, and I do—but silence swallows it whole. *What's happening to me?* I can only guess. Every part of me feels as if it's being burned away by some intangible, holy flame. As fast as the agony began, it ends, and the reaper withdraws his hand.

I drop to my knees, my head spinning at celestial speed as I catch my breath, reeling from the abrupt and sudden sense of relief. "What was that?" I gasp.

The reaper responds by rotating the blade of his scythe to my eye level. I glance up and I swear my heart stills in my chest. The reflection staring back at me in the smooth silver sheen of the metal is me, but not. I'm changed. *I'm ... like him!* My peachy human skin is gone, replaced by the same shifting, strangely transparent shadow flesh. My white skull is visible beneath it, and my eyes are dark hollows filled with black fire. My skull face grins back at me, and I reach up, running my skeleton hands through my hair. It's still there—long and rainbow—just as it was in life, only more vibrant!

Rising to my feet, I look to my soul mate. *"I'm like you,"* I say. Only the words don't come from my mouth. They speak directly from my mind to his.

"Not quite. You aren't an angel. Unfortunately, I don't have that kind of power, only He does... But as an archangel I have the authority to elevate a soul, ordaining one to greater ability and status. You are what we call an Ascended Spirit—a soul with a celestial purpose. It comes with the power to walk the hazy line between the worlds of the living and the dead," he says. *"So that you might act in the interests of the innocent and see justice done."*

I nearly fall over backward in sheer shock. *"You can speak? I can hear you. Oh my God!"* I tackle the reaper like a spider monkey, throwing my arms around his neck and wrapping my legs around his waist in excitement.

Mr. Grim smiles, and I can see him more truly now that we are akin. *"I can, indeed. We'll no longer have to rely merely on body language."*

I grin in return. "I don't know, I think we were able to connect pretty well on that basis."

The reaper laughs, his voice deep and enchanting. *"I believe a proper introduction of sorts is in order."*

Sliding down, I take a step back and cheerily offer my hand. *"Hi, I'm Renae Saltzman."*

"It's a pleasure to meet you, Renae. My name is Azrael, and I'm—as you guessed—the Angel of Death."

I squeal, bouncing on the spot. *"Azrael? Wow. I love it. And we're a thing, now, right? You and me? You promise?"*

Azrael takes my hand and places a surprisingly soft kiss upon it. *"We are bound, yes. I quite enjoy you."*

"Enjoy?" I query. *"Well, that's bloody*

romantic."

"As romantic as being bent over a fallen tree and fucked after dying?"

I don't know if my cheeks are capable of flushing pink anymore, now that I'm a different creature entirely, but I feel my heat rise. I bite my lip playfully. *"That was just fucking hot,"* I admit.

"It was," Azrael agrees. *"And, for the record, I kind of liked the whole Mr. Grim thing. It felt very taboo."*

"Is that so? More taboo than the Angel of Death taking a break from his duties to bone some random rainbow-haired trailer-park-trash?"

"You are no variety of trash, mate, and I won't allow you to say such things."

"Huh," I say, deviancy racing through my mind. *"Say I was to continue bad-mouthing myself, what exactly are you going to do about it, Mr. Grim?"*

"I'll show you."

****

In the next instant we're transported to an exceedingly epic Gothic cemetery. Mist hangs suspended just above the earth, and the moon shines brightly above, partially hidden by wispy, silver-limned clouds. Oak trees spread their shadows, obscuring the moonlight, and graves of all shapes and sizes litter the night-time landscape. Statues of great weeping angels stand guard over some, while others are marked by stone crosses. Impressive family mausoleums are also present, their decorative pitched rooves and pillars covered in lush, twisting ivy.

"Where are we?" I ask, trailing my fingers over the moss-laden headstones. *"It's beautiful."*

"A forgotten cemetery just outside of Salem," Azrael answers.

My jaw drops. *"You just blinked us to the other side of the fucking country? Just like that? Whoosh! And we're nearly three-thousand miles in the opposite direction?"*

"To be fair, we were between places. The domain of darkness is neither here nor there. But yes, I can travel wherever I choose. Wherever there is death, I go."

"Holy shit," I marvel. *"So, what were you going to show me, Mr. Grim?"* I ask, twirling in the darkness, admiring the way the moonlight reflects on my shadow flesh, creating a silver, shimmering sheen. I might be what they call an Ascended Spirit, but I feel like some kind of magnificent shadow faery!

Azrael closes the space between us and shrugs off his long, black cloak, revealing his beautiful, muscular body. Between his thighs his huge cock stands threateningly erect and ready for action. *"I'm going to show you the punishment you bring upon yourself for speaking so poorly of my chosen mate."*

"Is that so? And what if I enjoy it?"

"Then that'll further prove that you're my perfectly dark, little grim match."

"Little Grim? I like that." I purr over our telepathic connection, infusing my voice with as much seduction and lust as I can.

Chapter Eight

Azrael grabs my face, swooping down on me with incredible speed and ravenous need. Our long, flickering tongues dance, exploring each other's bodies in ways we haven't been able to—until now. His strong hands abandon my face to venture over my shadow form. He cups my breasts, squeezing and tweaking my black nipples.

I moan and let my head tilt back as his lips find the confluence of my neck and shoulder. He peppers my strange new skin with kisses before licking my throat, his tongue leaving a cool trail that tingles in its wake. *"Azrael,"* I whisper. *"I love you."*

My reaping angel nibbles my ear, his deathly cool breath sending shivers through me. *"And I love you, Renae."* In the next instant he lifts me up and lays me upon a low stone crypt, positioning himself between my raised legs. His mighty cock throbs, glistening under the radiance of the moon, sticky and wet with his pre-cum. *"You've been a wicked girl, Little Grim,"* he says, his voice firm. *"I'm afraid your sweet little Ascended ass is going to have to pay the price."*

Excitement and terror ripple through me and I lick my lips. *What will sex feel like with this new body?* I wonder. I'm about to find out. *"Please, Mr. Grim, fuck away my sin,"* I beg playfully.

"Your wish is my command, lover," he answers, as he rubs his thick head down my pulsing slit and to my puckered asshole. He teases me, slathering my starfish with his tasty chocolate essence. Stepping closer, he guides himself in against the noble resistance of my virgin hole.

In a heartbeat he breaches me. The pressure and slick heat of his cock stretching me wide makes my cunt pulse with desire. Holding onto my thighs, he drives forward, sinking his monstrous shadow cock right to the hilt. I scream, my strangled cry reverberating and echoing between our minds. *"Jesus Fucking Christ!"* I curse, my newly taloned fingers gripping the cold stone edge of the crypt. *"Are you sure I can't die twice?"*

Azrael thrusts again, his sac slapping against my cheeks. *"I'm certain, but it's sure as Hell going to feel like you can,"* he drawls in the most deliciously sinister way. And then he finds his stride and fucks my soul with an impossible supernatural rhythm. It's like being jackhammered by the biggest, most reliable automated fuck-machine in existence. He maintains a level of stamina no human man could ever hope to compete with, let alone match. I'm literally being fucked by an entity that is as much an angel as he is a beast and monster. And the sly, brooding bastard owns my heart, hook, line, and sinker.

I keen atop the crypt as the anal sex lasts beyond my wildest dreams. My poor pussy aches desperately, dripping down my lips to mix with the fluids squelching at my ass. I can't ignore it any longer. I've never been fond of touching myself, due to all the abuse at the hands of others. But now, I am whole and new, and my instinctual desires scream at me to play, to amplify my already otherworldly levels of pleasure to something entirely debaucherously wicked.

Sliding my hand over my body and smooth cunt, I find my clit and begin to rub, stroking and manipulating it between two fingers with a feverish hunger. The resulting sensations are unlike anything I've ever known. They fizzle through me, exploding inside of my body like a shaken bottle of soda. *"Oh my God!"* I cry out. *"What black magic is this?"* My back arches as the waves of my ecstasy envelop me, and Azrael moans—deep and throaty—as my ass clenches down hard, gripping and spasming around his cock like it has a mind of its own.

"Little Grim," he rasps, raising my ass and hooking my legs over his shoulders. *"You feel better than Heaven."*

My heart swells as every part of me throbs, rife with desire. Who could have guessed that I'd meet my soul mate in death on Halloween? I'd been looking for an escape, pure and simple, nothing more. I would have genuinely welcomed the embrace of the abyss. But discovering that Heaven and Hell truly exist, and that the Grim Reaper is my celestial mate? It's mind-shattering.

"I love you, Mr. Grim! Please come. It feels like you're going to kill me!"

Spurred on by my frantic begging and the mention of his pet name, Azrael pounds his way home, his skeleton hands digging into my hips as he uses me like a tight little cock-sheath.

Nonsensical murmurs and sobbing gasps shiver over our connection, and then like a pile-driver he impales my poor shadow ass one last time, burying his monster cock so deep it feels like it might pierce my fucking lungs. Then heat fills my hole, thick and creamy. There's so much, and he's so damn big, that it's forced to leak out my ass, around his beast, and onto the crypt beneath me, desecrating it in the most deliciously sacrilegious way imaginable.

I hang from his shoulders, spent and broken—my mind is blank, as if stuck on an old-school television test pattern. But one thought manages to snake through the haze of my pleasure-induced delirium. *"What a waste of chocolate!"*

Azrael gently lets me down, shuddering in the

wake of his own cosmic orgasm. *"I would have waited eternity for you, Renae Saltzman, but I'm glad I don't have to."*

The warmth of his love washes over me as I lie back in a mess of stickiness and bliss. As I stare up at the stars, a broad grin splits my skull face. *I'm never going to be alone again*, I realize. And I'll never be at the mercy of another sorry excuse for a man that reeks of stale piss and cigarettes. I'm the predator now, and I'm ready to reap justice of my own. Before All Hallows' Eve is over, I'm going to send some of those bastards that hurt me straight to Hell!

Chapter Nine

In the blink of an eye, we're back in the shit pit of Green Pines, and the thrill of the hunt fills me as thoroughly as Azrael's cum.

"Do you have someone in mind, love?" the reaper asks.

I grin. Oh, yes. I have someone in mind, all right. One of my mother's many ex-boyfriends. A particularly sick fuck who raped me with a beer bottle and put out his cigarettes on my hands when I was just thirteen years old. *"Troy Commons,"* I say. The name tastes sour even in my mind.

Azrael's presence seems to darken. His black feathered wings flare, and a chill emanates from him like an icy mist. He knows who I'm talking about, I have no doubt. He is the Angel of Death, after all, and I died ... meaning he likely knows me inside and out, all my secrets, all my flaws, and all of my shame.

"This way," I say, gesturing toward a small trailer with a faded red sunshade. The immediate area surrounding the mobile home is littered with beer bottles and cigarette butts. I shudder as the memory of my abuse resurfaces, and I can almost feel the sting of the circular burns on my skin, even though my new shadow flesh no longer bears the scars.

Stepping through the closed door of the trailer like a ghost, I find the fucker sucking on a bottle, slouched on the piss-stained, built-in couch. He stinks of stale cigarettes, and the walls are covered in tacky, torn-out magazine pornography. His long brown hair is matted, and his eyes are droopy with fatigue. The small television opposite him blasts some kind of ridiculous hillbilly reality show—idiots attempting stupid stunts in the country, like racing tractors, jumping off barns, and other physical stupidity.

Crawling up onto the couch beside him, I whisper into his ear. I remind him of all the terrible things he did to me—in detail—sharing how I felt, infusing my words with my own very real residual pain. *"You don't deserve to live,"* I say. *"You know that. You're a drunk, an abuser, a pedophile, and a rapist. You're an oxygen thief of the worst kind, and the world would be a better place without you in it."*

My abuser's eyes redden, and tears begin to flow. It almost sickens me to see him weep. Is he crying for the devastation he's wrought? For the harm he's inflicted? Or is he crying for himself—for the pathetic and disgusting excuse of a man he's become? I guess at the end of the day it doesn't matter. There's only one place he's going once he's a corpse, and that's straight through the portal to Hell.

The sicko reaches across the table, fumbling through weeks' worth of trash. In the next moment he has a handgun in his mouth, the barrel pointed directly at his brain. He seems to hesitate, on the brink of indecision, and it enrages me.

There won't be any denial. Not tonight, Troy. "Do it," I whisper. *"Now."*

The gun goes off, the explosive sound filling the trailer. He slumps down, lifeless, his brains painting the nicotine-yellowed walls behind him in a beautifully macabre display of red and mushy pink bits.

I squeal in delight, leaping up from the couch to dance on the spot. The sense of joy and relief I feel is profound. No woman or child will suffer ever again by his hand. I feel righteous and vindicated. I'm no longer his victim. I've taken back my power, and justice has finally been served.

"How does it feel?" asks Azrael as Troy Commons's soul manifests before us.

"Fucking epic!" I answer.

Troy's eyes bulge in terror when he lays his gaze upon us.

"Bye-bye, asshole," I hiss, flicking out my long, forked tongue, clawed hands resting on my shadowed hips. *"Say hi to Lucifer for me!"*

Azrael swings his scythe in an arc, slicing through Troy's mortally terrified soul. With a one-way ticket to Hell, he disappears in a swirl of black mist—his scream fading after him into the night. *"So,"* my angel drawls darkly. *"Who's next?"*

A hideously vicious grin stretches my lips. I feel more alive than ever before!

All Hallows' Eve blurs by, seemingly in the blink of an eye, and thirteen more bastards meet their demise, curiously by their own hand. Each of them will burn for their crimes, for all of eternity. The knowledge fills my Ascended heart with glee.

In a single night I've helped clean a county of a scourge that has been plaguing it for as long as I've existed. And I don't intend to stop here. The world is my oyster now. I intend to cleanse the Earth of its villains one damned soul at a time, for as long as is given to me.

****

The moon's light is waning, and the darkness is slowly receding, succumbing to the beautiful deep purple of the twilight before dawn. *"What happens now?"* I ask. *"What happens to me once the sun rises?"*

"You're not mist on a lake, Renae." Azrael laughs. *"You're not going to vanish with the first light. You're eternal now. Time no longer holds any sway over you."*

"So, we're a team?" I ask.

"We work together in our Divine purpose, lover, yes. And we will do so until the End of All Things. And hopefully, for humanity's sake, that won't be for a very long time."

"But when it does ... what then?" I ask, sudden and unexpected apprehension fizzing inside of me.

"Then we will have the right to choose our fate. We can choose to join God in his New Kingdom, or we can choose to simply un-exist."

"Un-exist?"

"When God finally destroys Hell, and all those within it, their souls will cease to be. They will be erased from the cosmos. Just gone, like a snowflake in a snowstorm—no more than a memory."

"Who would choose that?"

"I would," my reaper answers. *"When my duties are done, and all my centuries of Holy Service are spent, I'd like to just walk into the darkness and fade away, forever."*

"So, I couldn't convince you to join me in the New Kingdom, then?" I ask, shimmying my shoulders and jiggling my pert breasts suggestively.

"I have worked long already, my love. But if anyone could sway me, it would be you."

I grin, launching myself into my angel's arms. *"Then that's what I'll do. I'll spend the next however-long convincing you that an eternity of debauchery with me is infinitely preferable to just fading away."*

Chapter Ten

With a mischievous thought, I blink us back to the realm in-between, the shadowed domain of darkness where the portals of Heaven and Hell can be summoned.

Azrael shrugs off his long cloak and drops his scythe, standing bold in all his naked glory. *"You read my mind,"* he says, dark, heady allure emanating from his delicious form.

"You want to fuck like dogs in front of the portal to Heaven, too?" I ask incredulously.

"Yes. Yes, I do," he purrs.

"Hell, yes!" I grin, my skull face reflected back at me in Azrael's shadowy, and shimmering, shifting skin. *"But first, there's something I have to do,"* I say.

"And what's that?"

I drop reverently to my knees to stroke his monstrous cock, careful not to nick him with my talons. *"It's still technically Halloween,"* I say casually. *"And I haven't had my fill of treats!"* Azrael's beast gleams, pre-cum oozing from his head as if willed by my desire. *"Mm,"* I moan, as I lick him with my forked tongue. *"So fucking good."* I draw back then and look up into the dark hollows of my reaper's eyes. *"Why exactly does your cum taste like chocolate?"*

My angel shrugs. *"It's your guilty pleasure, isn't it?"* he answers simply.

Grinning again, I place a kiss on his slick slit. *"It was,"* I admit. *"But now you are. And I'm going to suck and fuck you until the night is done!"*

Taking Azrael into my mouth, I slither my serpentine tongue around his girth, jerking him as I bob my head back and forth. The Grim Reaper trails his long claws through my rainbow locks, and I sigh as electricity tingles over my scalp and a gloriously tangible shiver ripples down my spine. I don't know what it is, but there's just something about his special breed of domination that drives me wild. I've been dominated my whole life, but this isn't the same. This is liberation through submission.

I close my eyes as I make love to his cock with my mouth. I'm not merely fucking it to get him off. This is something much more intimate. He is the keeper of my heart, and his cock is the altar at which I will worship upon my knees.

Azrael growls across our connection, and I can feel the heat and desire transcending his physically spiritual form. His passion floods my senses, breaking over me like a furious white-crested wave crashing over a rocky shore. A gasp escapes me as every tender part of me begins to ache with need in response to his celestial pleasure. My nipples harden. My ass puckers, and my cunt contracts in wanting, wet with my own yearning.

I whimper around his cock as our mutual feelings overwhelm us. With his clawed grip tightening on my hair, the reaper takes matters into his own hands. Thrusting his beautifully defined hips, he shoves his monster down my dark throat mercilessly. I revel in his brutality. To feel so owned, so loved, and so used… *It's as close to Heaven as I ever want to be.*

My fingers stray between my legs, ignoring the mindless violence my mouth is being subjected to, and they seek out my own desperate ecstasy. Then, in a perfect moment of holy synchronicity, we reach climax at the same time. His delicious, thick, creamy milk chocolate cum spills down my throat as my pussy contracts, squirting its liquid love before the open portal of Heaven.

Azrael's load is more than I can handle. The sweet taste of Halloween leaks from my lips, spilling down my chin to drip between my bare breasts. Still hungry for more, I suck the reaper until he's dry. Looking up to him with the dark gaze of an excitable but sullen puppy who wants more, I tease my lip between my teeth.

The Angel of Death slaps me in the face with his cock, shoving me backward into the swirling black mist. Flipping me over as easily as if I were a feather, he lines up, gripping my hips, and plunges himself deep inside of me—driving the very air from my lungs.

"I love you, Mr. Grim," I gasp, every last nerve alive with ethereal fire.

"And I love you, Little Grim," he growls, digging his long, sharp claws into my soft shadow flesh.

With the ridiculously pristine beauty of Heaven just beyond, we fuck like wild dogs in heat in the darkness of the in-between—our moans of hallowed delirium echoing into eternity. And in the depths of my Ascended soul, I laugh with unbridled and debaucherous glee as the Grim Reaper rails me. *I'll never experience a Halloween quite like this one ever again!*

The End

FAEDRA ROSE

INFERNAL DESIRES

Loving Monsters, 3

Faedra Rose

Copyright © 2023

Chapter One

"With this blood I summon thee, Lucifer Morningstar, Fallen One, King of Hell, Bringer of Light, and Master of Truth." My voice is strong and unwavering as I chant alone in the middle of the forest. "Come to me on this Hallowed Eve, grant me your favor! Grant me my desires!" The lush forest falls silent as the candles of my circle are extinguished by a timely gust of brisk autumn wind.

I hold my breath, shivering in my simple white slip-dress beneath my black velvet cloak. The shadows loom and stretch around me, distorted by the dappled moonlight, reaching with gnarled fingers as if to ensnare the unwary.

For most, Halloween is nothing more than an excuse to overindulge in candy, wear risqué costumes, and run-amok … but for me it's so much more. Tonight represents sacred tradition, a duty passed down from mother to daughter since the time of the infamous Salem

Witch Trials. The foremother of our line paid with blood and flesh to save us all, to grant us protection, and to ensure we had a future beyond the cruelty and barbarism of those dark days.

The world has changed, and continues to change, but religious zealots still exist, and bigots of all kinds ravage the world with their hate-mongering. Inciting fear and panic among the masses on a daily basis, they ruthlessly corrupt from their untouchable positions of authority. And so, the truth remains that people have in fact not changed at all. Not really. The ill-informed are still as easily led, and stupid as sheep. They'll flock to the first false shepherd to promise prosperity, and rid them of their supposed enemies. And history has proven that time and time again my kind often fall prey to being viewed as just such an enemy.

And that's why I stand here tonight in my ceremonial circle of salt and flame, pantless and ready for what is to come. I must make the same sacrifice my forebears have made over the centuries if I am to ensure the renewal of our powers, and the safety of my great family. These powers I speak of are no sham. They are real, a gift from the Dark Lord, himself. All he asks in return is our fealty and love—quite literally. Soon, I will know the fiery touch of the Devil, and experience the depths of his depraved and infernal desires for myself.

The candles unexpectedly relight, bursting into flames one by one, until the circle is complete once more. A great fire erupts from the center of my makeshift altar on the forest floor, the flames spiraling upon themselves in a flurry, as if caught up in a great hurricane. The heat and wind buffets me, and I shield my eyes as the brightness diminishes.

There can be no mistaking the horrifyingly beautiful beast that now stands before me on cloven feet.

His pitch-black eyes gleam with the eternal darkness of the Abyss, like unholy jewels nestled into the face of an angel, his form more perfect than any likeness ever carved by the hands of man. Great curling horns like those of a ram sprout from his head—adding to his already unnatural height—and black hair spirals to his shoulders, drawing my attention to his long, braided goatee.

My breath catches in my throat as my gaze drops one painstaking inch at a time, drinking in the magnificence of his broad shoulders, chiseled abs, and the definition of the famed Triangle of Adonis that leads to the forbidden treasure resting beneath the silky black fur that covers his crotch and monstrous goats' legs.

"I've been expecting you," says Lucifer, his deep voice husky and full of illicit promise.

"Master," I breathe, falling to my knees, head bowed.

"What is your name, girl?"

Swallowing the urge to whimper, I clear my throat and raise my voice to just above a whisper. "It's Willow Wildes, Master. Daughter of Lily, granddaughter of Abigail."

"Ah, yes," he says. "I remember them most fondly. Each more than earned their power." Lucifer pauses a moment, before squatting and lifting my chin with a long, curved claw. "And now you seek your own power," he says. "As the women of your line have done for some three-hundred years."

I tremble as I gaze into the eternity of his dark eyes. "Yes, Master. I have come to offer you blood and flesh in return for your favor, just as Sarah did so long ago."

"You are a unique beauty, Willow Wildes," he says thoughtfully. "I have not seen this for over a hundred years." Raising my chin further, he brushes away errant strands of my blood-red hair to examine my face. "One blue, and one green, for the sky above and the earth below. Most intriguing."

"It's a condition. We call it heterochromia," I whisper.

"It is a good and rare omen," the Devil interjects. "It bodes well for you, my pretty. To be different is a gift in and of itself. To wear your difference with pride, and stand apart from others as unique takes courage."

"I only ask for that which my foremothers were given," I say as he rises.

"I cannot give you the powers of your foremothers," he answers, looking down upon me.

Fear and sudden panic surge in the pit of my stomach, bringing with it the sour taste of bile. I wring my hands in my lap in an effort to contain my nerves and maintain my self-control. *Dare I question the Dark Lord?* I lick my lips, my gaze fixed on his cloven hooves. "Have I offended you, Master?"

"No, child."

Heart racing, I feel like I'm going to be sick. "Am I unworthy?"

"Far from it."

"Then why?" I ask, looking up to gaze upon his flawless face backlit against the bright moon.

"You have been marked for greatness, Willow. I cannot give you that which I have given your foremothers because you are destined to have much greater powers."

"Greater?" The word tumbles from my lips unbidden in wonder.

"Much greater," he emphasizes.

With chaotic butterflies in my belly, I place my hands on my knees—palms facing up in submission and obedience—and hold his gaze as boldly as I'm able. "Ask of me what you will, Master, and it will be yours."

Chapter Two

"First," says Lucifer, a smile upon his lips. "Blood."

"Of course," I mutter under my breath, chastising myself. *It should have been my first thought!* Reaching for my athame, I bare my palm. Then, recalling to mind the words inked into my family's ancient grimoire, I take a deep breath. "Master, I pledge my eternal soul to you, and with this blood sacrifice I willingly give of my service, fealty, love, and devotion." I wince as I press the tip of the ceremonial dagger to my palm, and drag the blade across my skin. It cuts smoothly, like a warm knife through butter. Grimacing, I cup my hands together so that the blood might well there, and fill like a chalice of living flesh.

"Accept this offering, Great Master, and I will be forever in your debt. I will become your blood bride, and take of no man's seed but your own. I will fulfill your every infernal desire, and bear your offspring in spite of God. I will raise them in the Old Ways, so that they might know you, love you, and come to you when it is their time."

The Devil cups his hands beneath mine, and raises me to my feet. When I am standing, he stares into my very soul, and I shiver with anticipation under his intense gaze. "Your offering is accepted," he says, before stooping down to drink my blood and seal our pact. When he is done, he smiles, his teeth stained red. Then licking his lips in the most breathtakingly salacious way, he runs a single curved claw over my wound, cauterizing it with Hellfire. "This scar will serve as a reminder of your pledge, and of what we share from this day forward."

He releases my hand and I tentatively touch the long scar. The pain is gone, though the mark will remain forever. "Thank you, Master. What would you ask of me this Hallowed Night?"

"I will have you in all ways imaginable, and beyond, my pretty. I hunger for your flesh, and I will be sated. Now, on your knees."

I sink to my knees again with a niggling suspicion of what's to come. *Thank the Morningstar, I'm not a virgin.* I've practiced for this night, as my mother and grandmother instructed I should. The Devil does not glorify virginity. He sees no value in the untried and desireless. Instead, he values a strong sense of Self, and the boldness to go after that which you desire.

"Suck my cock with that pretty little mouth of yours," he commands. Trailing one hand across his groin, he reveals a monster of frightening size. I wiggle my ass, and clench my cunt internally as I bite my lip. *It's fucking huge!* Gawping at it in open awe, I swallow hard. It's the size of my bloody forearm. *Holy shit.* I shuffle forward across the damn earth, releasing the sweet odor of decay into the air as I tentatively take hold of Lucifer's cock.

I'm holding the Devil's dick. Fuck! Opening my mouth, I dance my tongue across his gleaming head, circling its immense girth. *This thing is going to split me in half.* I begin to panic. *Be calm. Just focus,* I remind myself. *You're not the first Wildes to ride this pony, and you won't be the last.* The Dark Lord's cock is smooth, and he's cut—*or was he created without foreskin?* I never thought to ask that of my foremothers…

"You humans really are delightful," purrs Lucifer, tangling his claws in my hair. "It never ceases to amaze me just how small and fragile you are. Just look at you … such a good girl," he praises. "That's it. Take in as much as you can, sweetheart. I want you to try and suck the

Hellfire out of me."

Opening my gob as wide as I can, I bob my head forward and take him to the back of throat, gagging almost instantly. It's like trying to fit a whole footlong in your mouth. It's so thick that it fills me from floor to roof, cheek to cheek. There is no wiggle room for my tongue at all. I glance up at him, eyes watering as he moans, and a sting whispers across my scalp as he grips a fistful of my hair too tightly. I wince and whimper, tears leaking down my cheeks despite my best efforts to hold them back.

"Oh, Willow. Is it too big for you? Too much to work with?" The timbre of his ancient angelic voice sends shivers through me, and causes dampening between my inner thighs.

I daren't agree. Pleasing the Devil is all that stands between me and the power I need to protect my family—the power I deserve. I shake my head with my mouthful, and Lucifer laughs with good-natured humor.

"Sweet girl. You're determined, aren't you?" The Fallen angel rocks his hips, and his cock moves just enough for me to catch my breath and readjust my jaw. "I like a strong spirit," he continues. "An unbreakable will is something I prize above all else." Taking hold of both sides of my head, he offers me a beautiful, seductive, and darkly unapologetic smile. "I'm going to fuck your face, now, Willow. And I'm going to spill my first load of hot seed all over your pretty pouty face. Is that understood?"

As best I'm able to, I nod, and brace myself for what will no doubt be the most brutal cock onslaught my poor mouth will ever experience. Relaxing my throat, I tilt my head back further, and hold my master's gaze. His devilish grin is to-die-for. There's just something about those fangs resting against his full lower lip that has me aching to kiss him, and feel the sharp prick of those pearly whites at my throat.

Chapter Three

Cock fills my throat, delving much deeper than I ever thought possible. He saws back and forth, taunting me, making light of just how much of a struggle this is for me. *But then, I guess, that's half the fun.* The Devil revels in games of control, in deals made, and pacts struck. I signed up for this of my own choice. No one forced me. The burden of tradition weighs heavily upon me, that much is true, but even so ... I could have chosen to stray from the well-trod path of my family. *But I chose this fate because I want it.*

Satan is my master, and even if we are granted infinitely more freedoms than God would ever permit, we are still ultimately his servants. Though the trade of one's immortal soul is fair in the minds of most. A sacrifice for power. A straight exchange. What does God give? Silence. Not love. Not protection. Nothing but a book of dogmatic rules and an eternity of silence. He might as well not exist at all—it certainly seems like we scarcely exist to Him. He would have let my foremothers burn and hang. But not Lucifer. He is the savior of my great line, and for this, I will gladly pay the blood price.

My poor throat spasms around the Fallen angel's cock, and my eyes continue to water, my physical exertion streaming down my cheeks like hot tears. He fucks my face as if I were no more than a puppet of flesh, and it is both demeaning and entirely arousing. As my eyes burn, and I repeatedly gag—drool unceremoniously pouring from the sides of my mouth—my fingers find their way between my wet thighs. I can't help it. Being used by the Dark Lord is an honor, and it's hot as Hell.

Lucifer's animalistic moans spur me on, and I pleasure myself on the forest floor of Salem like a common whore. My own frantic sounds of ecstasy soon escape me, trembling around the Devil's dick to be heard.

"Yes," Lucifer growls. "Come for me, my pretty slut. Show me how much you want this." Pumping harder, he forces my face against the dark hair of his crotch. Again, and again, my lips hit his base, and he holds me there on the precipice of darkness—luxuriating in the way my body fights, so desperate to eject him from my tight airway.

My vision begins to dim, and I see stars, or rather, floating sparkles. And I know he's pushing my limits. Erotic asphyxiation is one of my darkest kinks, and the thought of being fucked like a piece of meat, then passing out with a mouthful of Fallen cock drives me to the brink of orgasm. Then in a mind-blowing moment of clarity Lucifer withdraws completely, and as a lungful of cold autumn air fills me, his cum sprays my face like a fucking fire hose.

I close my eyes and it drips into my mouth. My rhythm reaches a fever pitch and I shudder violently as the force of my own release tears through me. My master's cream spills down my chest, sticky and thick, causing the thin white fabric of my dress to adhere to my full breasts. My rock-hard nipples strain against the sheer material proudly.

"Now, eat it up," he instructs as I try to catch my breath. I vaguely lick my cum-splattered lips, and Lucifer shakes his head. "Not like that. On your back, my beauty. You're not the only one who's hungry."

Through the haze of my lust-fueled delirium I roughly lower myself back onto the leaf-strewn earth, knees up, legs spread wide. *Oh, my God.* And just like that the Devil is between my thighs, chowing down on my soaked minge like a starved madman. I writhe against his wicked mouth, completely under his spell.

"Eat," he commands, this time directly to my mind.

I moan as he doesn't miss a beat, then using my fingers I wipe congealing cum from my heated cheeks, before slipping them into my mouth and sucking them clean.

"Good girl, swallow my Hellseed."

I continue to wipe and suck, my hot tongue wrapping around my fingers as Lucifer's flicks around my clit with vicious precision. I want to scream. The pressure inside me builds again. It's almost more than I can bear. His long tongue penetrates me, twisting and vibrating as if it had a life of its own. "Fucking Christ!" I swear, my hands straying over my cum-soaked breasts, and towards the ache beneath my navel that burns brighter with each spent breath. *"Oh, Lucifer. Master. I can't hold on!"*

"You can. And you will. You are here to please me, my scarlet-haired pretty. You will obey," he purrs with an edge of menace.

I manage to clean my face of cum, as ordered, but not even the taste of the Devil's cold spaff can pull me back from the precipice of ecstasy. I ride it like a woman bound above a sawhorse, on the tips of my toes, back arching, straining with all my might to hold back, to not let go. I sob, crying out. "Please, Master. I beg you!" I sink my teeth into my lower lip until pain blossoms— anything to distract me, to momentarily keep from letting go. The metallic tang is jarring, yet familiar.

With real tears of anguish and frustration streaming from my eyes, I try to squeeze my thighs closed, clenching Lucifer's horned head between them. He ramps up his wicked ministrations and I scream, my voice rending the otherwise silent night like a blade. I've never felt so intensely sensitive in my entire life. It's like he knows just how to piss upon the line dividing pleasure and pain. *"Mercy, Master!"* I cry out in my mind.

"Now," says the King of Hell.

His command shivers through me and I let go. Like a dam breaking, the fire within me explodes with enough force to steal the breath from me. I curl my toes in the damp soil and gasp as wave after wave of electricity assaults me—frying every last nerve—until I'm utterly spent. Lucifer sits back, admiring his handiwork. His sinful smile makes my very soul squirm inside of me, and then, as my muscles slowly start to relax, and breathing comes more easily, a tidal wave of physical fatigue crashes over me and I slip into blissful oblivion.

Chapter Four

I open my eyes to find Lucifer staring down on me intently, the glow of the All Hallows' moon behind him creating the illusion of a bright angelic halo.

"Welcome back," says the Fallen angel, his black eyes full of mirth as a smile quirks his sexy lips.

"I passed out?" I ask. I lick my lips to wet them, before allowing him to help me to a sitting position.

"You did."

I grin.

"You like that, do you, my pretty?"

I shrug, suddenly aware of my now crispy, cum-drenched dress. "As much as I enjoy being independent, and strong ... I like to be dominated when it comes to sex."

"You're not afraid to speak your mind, Willow. I like that."

I feel my cheeks flush with heat. "I've learned from a long line of strong women," I answer as I untie my cloak. It whispers to the forest floor behind me. Rising to my feet, I lift my destroyed dress over my head and drop it without a second thought. "For what it's worth," I say, standing before the Devil as bare as the day I was born, "you're not nearly as terrifying as I've been led to believe."

"Is that so?" says Satan too softly.

I take a step back, immediately regretting my choice of words. "I didn't mean..." I stammer. "I just think you're beautiful—for a monster."

"Oh, my darling girl. You like to dance with danger, don't you?"

Fuck. Fuck. Fuckity. Fuck. Fuck! "I mean, yes, but also ... I meant no offense, Dark Lord. I worship you.

I want you as you are. I just meant that the whole world is terrified of you, and I don't understand it."

"So, you want to understand, is that it? Do you want to see my dark side, Willow? Because this isn't it. Not by a long shot, precious."

"You don't need to prove anything to me, Master. Forgive my brazen tongue."

Lucifer closes the space between us, until I'm forced to crane my neck back to look at him. "Answer my question," he whispers dangerously.

"Have any of my forebears seen your dark side?" I ask, holding my breath as I await his answer.

Lucifer's smile is as sinister as it is swoon-inducing. "No, none have been so unwise, or so bold as to wish for it."

Fuck me. Despite every single internal instinctive alarm bell screaming at me to back the fuck up and grovel for forgiveness, I ignore them all. Survival be damned. Nothing matters in this moment as much as my curiosity, my sense of rebellion, and my desire to prove myself as strong enough to handle the Devil at his worst. "Then, yes," I say. "I want to see."

The Dark Lord steps back, and turns from me, his black tail swishing from side to side. "Just remember you asked for this," he says over his shoulder.

Steeling myself for what's to come, I stand my ground and watch his back intently.

My master bursts into flame. It writhes over his form like a living thing, licking, and caressing, enveloping him like an infernal lover. I startle as immense webbed wings burst from between his shoulders, and when he stretches them out beneath the moonlight, I see that they are torn, with gruesome holes riddling the dark membranes. His horns straighten and twist, while his cloven hooves become clawed feet. His goat-legs lose their glossy pelt of black fur, replaced with thick, red, ropey, knotted muscles that look gnarled and deformed—both pockmarked by hideous decay, and half-melted at the same time. Burnished red scales dot his form haphazardly, as if perhaps he were once entirely scaled, but now only the remnants of that great draconic legacy remain.

My stomach lurches as it seems his very form steams, the whorls of vapor dancing against the night sky. A long, snakelike tail whips back and forth, protruding from the base of his spine, above his scarred ass. Its tip appears sharp like an arrow, pointed as if it could be used as a weapon to stab or lacerate. A shudder runs through me, but I hold fast. *I will not show fear*, I tell myself. *This is my master. I will be reverent, and I will not cower.*

"Are you ready to see me as I am, Willow Wildes? Marred as I am by my Fall into the Void, and burned as I was cast into the Pit?" he asks, his voice deeper and rougher, the beautiful lilt long gone—as if his very throat has been torn asunder and left to heal without care. "This is the price I paid for standing against our Heavenly Father. This is what becomes of those who refuse to obey." Lucifer turns, flaring his wings as he does, and my heart drops.

"Oh, Master," I whisper, my hands flying to my mouth in shock and dismay. "What has He done to you?" Lucifer's angelic face is scaled, and his black eyes are deep-set, a heavy brow overhanging their inner fire. His mouth is something born directly from a child's nightmare. He has no lips. *Were they torn off, or melted away? Or were they removed by God himself for the crime of his supposed lies?* I wonder.

His teeth are fangs, and a forked tongue flicks behind them. Despite the hints of great strength in his form and bearing—perfectly ripped muscles and broad shoulders—he is the embodiment of pain, rage, and despair. Behind the terror of his outward appearance, a deep well of pain emanates from him in almost tangible waves.

"What do you see?" asks the Fallen angel, taking a step closer.

I lick my lips, and suppress the bile of revulsion that threatens to surge up my throat. My gaze wanders over his form as words momentarily fail me. *Sweet Dark Lord!* In this form Satan wields two fucking cocks, one beneath the other, both as cunt-clenchingly huge as the other. Unlike his satyr cock which was dark, smooth, and attractive, these cocks are hideously scarred and ridged with contortions of flesh. "Master," I choke out. "What are you?"

"I am what I have always been, my child. I am the dragon that set the Throne of God afire. The behemoth whose wings cast a shadow over the Realm of Eternal Light. I am the Devil, the Dragon, and the Angel of Music and Light. I am the Liar, the Deceiver, the Beast, and the Damned. I am the King of Man, and the Enemy of the Lord on High."

"And this was the price?" I ask, trembling as he draws ever nearer. "This is the price of your freedom? Our freedom? You saw that God was setting us up for failure from the start, didn't you—ever since Eden—and you stood for us, you took our side, even though you knew what it would cost you…"

Lucifer reaches out to caress my face with one immense, clawed hand. "Now you see, my pretty. Free will comes at a great cost, and if you do not choose His Path, then this is what awaits you. I am His warning to mankind."

Chapter Five

"God would cast you out," says Lucifer. "For you're all sinners in his eyes. He damned his own children with their very first breaths. But I would never do such a thing. I have always embraced mankind for all that it is—beautiful, flawed, reckless, ugly, loyal, and cruel. You are perfect in your imperfection. You are whole. Both Light and Dark. He does not see that we must be both, and so he has made an enemy of me, when we ought to be partners in this Grand Design."

"Would you truly love me, Master, even if I failed you? Even if I betrayed you?" I ask, as I lean into his warm hand.

"Always. It is God who doesn't know the mercy of forgiveness, Willow. In my world chances spring eternal. My creed is redemption. Hell is for all those who refuse to be slaves to a tyrant. Hell is the Kingdom of the Free. There are no rules, no laws. There is no need for them. The chaos balances itself—has a way of finding its own level. And I sit above it all, a just king who understands sins and the temptations of the flesh better than anyone."

"You saved my family," I whisper, looking up into his dark gaze. "And for that, I will always be grateful. You gave us life, when God condemned us to death. His zealots were baying for blood, the nooses already strung…" I shudder internally as I'm assaulted with an ancestral memory. "Ask of me anything you desire, Master, and it will be yours," I reiterate. "You are truly beautiful. I see it more clearly now than ever before."

The Devil's forked tongue darts past his fangs, licking at the air where the flesh of his lips ought to be. "I have not had physical pleasure in this form since Lilith was exiled from Eden," he says. "Not even the whores of Hell like to see me this way. Even darkness prefers beauty, it would seem. I can't blame them—I know I do."

The note of sadness in his voice sets my heart ablaze, and I know without doubt what I need to do next. "Then I will be like Lilith," I say boldly. "I will have you as you are, for who you are. You are humanity's champion and I would have you claim me as your own—body, mind, and soul, Master."

Satan visibly shivers at my declaration, his great brutalized wings flexing against the moon. "Do you mean that, precious?" he asks, slowly dragging a claw down between my breasts to my navel, leaving a razor-thin red trail that blossoms beads of crimson. "I yearn for you to give me everything that you are, but I will not take it without your willing desire."

"I desire you, Lord Satan," I say, catching his free hand and placing a kiss upon its marred flesh. "Fuck me as you fucked the Queen of Demons so long ago. Don't hold back. Give me all that you are…"

"Oh, my pretty. You can't comprehend what it means to hear you say such a thing." Lucifer growls, then moves to spin me around—I imagine so that we might fuck like dogs—but I raise my hand, laying it against his spectacularly defined abs.

"No, Master," I say. "I'm not afraid. I wish to look into your eyes as you sheath me. I want you to use me like a puppet of flesh, and watch as you lose yourself in the pleasure of it. Hold me. Fuck me until I don't know where I begin, and you end."

Reaching under me, Lucifer slathers both of my holes with his ample, oozing pre-cum. Careful, so as not to cut me this time, he trails his fingers between my puffy and aching cunt lips, and then circles my puckering starfish. "You are human, and this will hurt at first, my pretty. But I will do for you what I can." My master whispers words of an unknown language under his breath, and I feel suddenly and inexplicably more relaxed, as if every muscle in my body has been pampered and kneaded into blissful, soft pliancy.

"What was that?" I ask, marveling at how I feel as incredible as a pile of gooey, melted caramel.

"Sorcery. Magic. Call it what you will. I have used words of power to soothe and limber your body, so that you're more able to accommodate me and less likely to suffer damage, little one."

I nod in understanding as he lifts me by my waist in his enormous hands, and lowers me onto both his cocks. I gasp in unexpected need as I feel their heads make contact with my hot, wet holes. "Oh, Master," I breathe, as he slides me on more easily than I ever dreamed feasible, sheathing his great beasts inside of me inch by thick breathless inch. Despite the words of power, I panic as I gaze down at the sheer size of his dual beasts disappearing inside of me. "I'm going to split in half!" I instinctively clench in an effort to save my insides from sundering.

"The worst is over, precious," Satan coos with his rough, gravelly voice, his hands vise-tight on my waist.

Focusing on my breathing, I try to relax my mind, but fail dismally as my ass and cunt stretch agonizingly slowly in protest to the supernatural invasion, forced wider than they've ever been made to before. His cocks seem to penetrate me for an eternity as I am slid down him like a mere condom of human flesh. For a moment my eyes roll back in my head, and the brilliance of the All Hallows' moon blinds me. There's nothing but cock. It impales me, consumes me—is me.

Mortal fear continues to permeate my thoughts. *If*

he pushes himself all the way to the hilt, he might pierce my bloody lungs! In my mind I visualize his cocks tearing me apart, blood gushing from every conceivable orifice. I can almost hear the squelching, and the echo of my own screams as my life gushes out of me in a gory shower of dark scarlet. I feel fire, and the brutal, continuous snap of bone. Then in an infernal blast Satan replaces my blood with thick, creamy cum, but it's not enough to hold me together, and I slough away, dripping between his fingers to the forest floor like the pulpy remnants of a monster's meal.

Chapter Six

"Willow."

I hear my name like a whisper on the wind. It caresses my mind, soothing my heart like a summer breeze.

"Willow."

And suddenly I'm back, alive, and entirely whole. My fears overtook me, consuming me like the flames of Hell, seeking to drown me in doubt and betrayal. But now they are gone—banished back to where they belong by my terrifying, possessive winged Devil.

"You have a dark and beautiful mind," he says, as he strokes my cheek with the back of his scarred knuckles.

I feel a surprising coolness beneath me, and notice we're now on the forest floor, my Master buried deep inside me, his dark eyes regarding me with a mix of concern and amusement.

"I would not break you, little one," he says, flicking his forked, snakelike tongue over my nose and lips. "The line between pleasure and pain dances upon a knife's edge, and there I like to play. But I would never destroy you. I desire to keep you."

I nod as I regain my bearings, and Lucifer slowly thrusts forward, building his two-cocked rhythm once again.

"Oh, my God," I swear, my hand flying to my mouth, my eyes instantly wide. Every single stroke feels indescribably incredible, and I curl my toes in the damp earth in response. "What have you done, Master?" I gasp.

My monster grins, never dropping a single note of his delicious melody inside me.

Then the obvious hits me, like a bolt of lightning

from above straight to my throbbing, oversensitive clit. It's music pulsating in me—through me. *Sweet Dark Lord, it's music!* Lucifer was the Archangel of Light and Music. *He's playing me like an instrument, creating a song that only we can share.*

"Our song is like no other," he breathes, pumping me further into the dirt with the wild and frantic energy of a storm raging over a tempestuous sea. "This ecstasy is more than Heaven ever could be. For this gift of Service, I will make a queen of you, Willow Wildes. A Grand Witch, a Priestess of Hell. You will be my Eternal Paramour."

His words wash over me, almost tangibly, like soft feathers tickling over my skin and hard nipples. I moan, lost in lust and devotion. "I never knew sex could feel like this," I say, each word timed to a viciously brutal thrust.

"This is Forbidden," Satan growls. "That's why it feels so good. Our coupling is an Unholy affront to the Creator, himself. And nothing could feel better."

I grasp as fistfuls of colored leaves, shaking my head from side to side as I do. "It's too much," I whimper. "Master, it's too much. I can't endure it!"

"You can bear it, my pretty, and you will." The Devil milks my mortal tightness for all its worth, reveling in the way my small frame writhes beneath him, gripping his cocks as if they were literal lifelines out of the Void. "Do you trust me, Willow?" he asks, his voice like thunder.

"I do," I sulk against the unfathomable pleasure assaulting my soft, full form.

Satan leans down, wrapping his great arms under me so that his weight is balanced on his elbows. His gleaming eyes fill my vision. "You are mine," he says. "Now, and forever." And I get my wish. I feel the sharp prick of his fangs as they sink into my neck. It's an entirely different pain, and I cry out as he continues to fuck me. My hands trail over his marred, muscular shoulders as I feel warmth spill over my breast.

He's drinking my blood, I realize, like the vampires of urban myth. His bite is crushing—like a mechanical vise—and I reel. Mindless in the immeasurable agony, pleasure, and darkness that lays itself upon me, blanketing my senses until there's nothing left in the world but the sound of my own heart pulsating and pumping valiantly in my ears.

Just when it feels as though the Abyss will claim me, and I'll join my foremothers in Hell, Lucifer withdraws, sealing the gaping wound in my throat with a breath of Hellfire. The scent of my searing flesh fills my nostrils and I gag, still so close to death that I can taste it.

Satan pulls one arm from under me, and my head tips back, resting over his forearm. Biting his wrist, it begins to bleed, and his blood is black. "Drink of my cursed blood, child," he instructs. "Claim your right to greatness, and lifetimes of ecstasy beyond your wildest imaginings." He presses the dripping gash to my lips.

I grasp at his arm and tongue the wound, encouraging his ink-black blood to fill my mouth. It spills over the edges of my lips to trail down my face. It tastes like ambrosia, or at least what I imagine the ancient food of the Greek gods to taste like. Sweet and hot, it burns a molten path down my throat like liquor on a cold evening.

I splutter, coughing as his wound continues to pour. "Too much." I gasp, choking.

My master seals his self-inflicted wound, scooping me up from the ground—still mounted—so that he's standing once more. "Come with me, my queen," he whispers as I catch my breath. His thrusting pulverizes what little is left of me, until I can no longer differentiate between my ass and my cunt. There's just endless sensation. It blurs together, and I have what I desired. I have no idea or sense of where I begin, and where he ends. Joined by the flesh—carnal and infernal, unholy and sacrilegious—we are bound by blood and lust.

As I bounce upon Lucifer's cocks the ecstasy grows to an unbearable crux, and I feel my entire being begin to quiver and shake in his grasp. "Oh, Master!" I gasp on the cusp of oblivion.

"Come with me. Now." He snarls like a savage beast.

A string of garbled, noncoherent obscenities spills from my lips, drowned out by my own moans and cries. Lucifer thrusts twice more before he stiffens under me. His beautifully nightmarish face contorts, and a horror-inducing roar fills the night, driving watchful owls and nesting bats from the trees. The sound is unearthly and demonic in every possible sense. Temporarily deafened, I close my eyes and narrow my focus to my own body.

I tangibly feel his hot release fill me like a volcano erupting inside of an enclosed cavern. I come around him violently in response. Our combined cum oozes from me, sweet and thick, to form a sticky, congealing waterfall down my thighs and ass crack. I shiver in the aftermath of our shared orgasm, before my fragile mortal form gives up on me.

Utterly spent, I turn to jelly in my master's arms. Leaning against his broad chest, breathing in the heady scent of our sex, and the smell of his hot demon flesh, I give into the alluring embrace of darkness, again.

Chapter Seven

A bright glow awakens me, filtering through my lashes to rouse my consciousness. I open my eyes, blinking against the light. The glow slowly diminishes until I can see clearly and my breath catches in my throat. "Lucifer," I say. My master kneels over me—and he's the single most beautiful man I've ever seen. With searing eyes of sapphire starlight, long hair the color of midnight, a chiseled jaw, high cheekbones, and generous lips ... he is without doubt the most perfect creature God ever created.

"God must weep for your absence," I whisper as Lucifer reaches down to stroke my cheek.

His white wings flare behind him, glittering in the moonlight with stardust and the whispers of dreams. "He made his choice," he answers. "As I made mine. A child cannot linger in their father's shadow forever."

"I don't feel worthy to see you like this," I say from the forest floor.

"You, above all others, are worthy," he says. "You've proven that."

My brow furrows and I offer the Devil a wry smile. "All I did was love you."

"Which is more than most."

I sigh into his hand, basking in the radiance of his divine beauty.

"Are you ready, Willow Wildes?"

"For what, Master?"

"To become the Devil's Bride, of course."

My mind falls out of my ass and I lay there like a stunned mullet. I don't know how much time passes between his first words and his next, but I feel so utterly breathless and overwhelmed that I forget how to tangibly function.

"On your knees," he instructs.

The calming timbre of his voice soothes me, bringing me back to the moment, and I comply without thought, as if in a trance. *Lucifer wants to marry me?* The words play over and over like a broken record in my head. How could an angel—a perfect being—want to be with me? "I don't understand," I utter, gazing up at him. "I came tonight to honor the oath of my forebears, and to receive the powers promised. What does it mean to be your bride, Master? Is it a ceremonial title?"

"Lilith was my first bride," he answers. "And I have not taken another since. Thousands of years have passed, and I've been watching. Waiting. Searching. For just the right woman. I yearn to grow my harem, Willow. I would have you be my Second Wife, mother to my offspring, and a true Queen of Hell. When your mortal days are spent, you will join me, and rule by my side upon a throne of your very own."

"I—" I can scarcely fathom the thought, let alone speak the words aloud. "You would have me at your side, a sister-wife to Lilith, Queen of Demons?"

"I would," he says. "I need a harem of thirteen brides for when the time of Revelations comes. Each one an incredibly strong woman of her own merit, with her own unique qualities. And I will treasure you all as the sacred jewels in my crown. You will be my warrior queens, commanders of legions, who will ride with me onto the battlefield at the End of Days."

"Holy shit," I blanche.

Lucifer laughs, and the sound is music to my ears. "So, will you accept, Willow Wildes? Will you be my bride and queen? Will you reign with me in Hell over the Dark Court?"

Tears stream unbidden from my eyes and I nod

emphatically, not a single doubt in my mind. "I will, Master. I accept."

Lucifer smiles, manifesting a blood-red jewel in the air between us. "This is one of the thirteen tears that God wept when I rebelled. It is one of my crowning jewels, and I would anoint you with it."

"It would be an honor," I whisper. The tear-shaped jewel floats toward me—defying gravity—and with only a small searing sensation that makes me wince, it sets itself neatly into the flesh above my brow.

"Rise, my queen," says the flawless angel.

I stand, barefoot on the leaf-littered earth, sky clad and covered only in a splattered mixture of our blood and cum. "Is this real?" I ask, a shiver rippling through me.

"Indeed, it is. How do you feel?"

I lick my lips and think a moment. "I feel powerful," I say as the realization dawns upon me. "I can't explain it, I just feel different somehow."

"That's because you have been gifted your power, my sweet witchling. Magic as you understand it, is now at your disposal."

A grin leaps to my face and I narrow my gaze. "Really?" I ask. "How?"

"My blood," he explains. "Try something. Anything."

Holding out my hand, palm toward the star-spangled sky, I focus on what I desire. "Fire," I command. Flames erupt from my skin, dancing over my fingers, its many tongues licking greedily at the brisk night air. "Oh, Master!" I crow like a giddy child on Halloween with a sack full of candy. Dancing on the spot, I watch, rapt as the flames continue to burn in my grasp—all the while I remain entirely unharmed.

"And that's just the beginning," says Lucifer, a note of pride in his voice. "You are the greatest witch of your line, Willow Wildes Morningstar. Your powers know no limit but those you impose upon yourself."

I blink, extinguishing the fire with a thought, and do a double-take. "Did you just say Willow Wildes Morningstar?"

"You're my wife, aren't you?"

"Holy fucking shit!" I squeal. "My family is going to freak out!" Throwing myself into my husband's arms, heedless of the blood and sticky mess that I am, I wrap my arms around his neck, holding him tight. To my great relief the Morningstar humors me, embracing me fondly in return—spinning me around in the forest. I feel giddy with joy and awe, and glutted with the supernatural power now coursing through my veins.

"Are you happy, my queen?" he asks when he sets me down.

"Positively ecstatic," I exclaim with a grin, before snaring his beautiful angelic lips in a passionate kiss. He tastes like sin, and honeyed liquor. His kiss has me reeling, and I moan against him as his fingers trail through my long hair, while his free hand possessively grasps the swell of my shapely, ample ass.

Chapter Eight

Lucifer ends our kiss, withdrawing gently. "Willow, there is something that needs to be said."

I lick my lips at the unexpected shift in the moment, and the serious, seemingly apologetic expression on his face. "What is it, Master?" I ask, my heart skipping with concern.

"This will be the first and last time you see me until your time here is done."

I stare up into his sapphire blue eyes, trying desperately to swallow the lump that's formed in my throat, making it suddenly hard to breathe. "I know," I whisper. "I mean, I realize. I know you only saw my forebears the once, on All Hallows' Eve, to grant their powers and bless them with your seed…"

"If I could, I would see you more often, but I'm not God. I can't be everywhere at once. Hell needs its King, and there is much to be done before the End of Days," he explains.

I wipe away a traitorous tear. "Of course. I understand completely," I say, my chest aching with each word.

"You will have an incredible mortal life, my queen," he says, stroking my cheek. "You will birth me twins, and they will be blessed with your strength. They will need your guidance in this broken world. But when they are grown, if there truly comes a day when you can no longer stand to be here, summon me on All Hallows' Eve, and I will come. I'll claim you and relieve you of this mortal coil once and for all."

My lips tremble, and I sniffle back the rest of my tears. "Twins?"

"They'll be the greatest offspring I will have

spawned since creating the first demons with Lilith. You will be proud, Willow," he assures me. "Don't lament my absence. Revel in your power, in your earthly freedom, and live for what's to come. Hell awaits its new queen, as I will. And one day, when my harem is complete, you will have a dozen sisters with whom to share your endless life—and you will be closer than blood could ever be. And together, we will have eternity, Willow."

I shiver at his words. "An infernal coven."

"You will be the most powerful women in this universe. The angels in Heaven will tremble to behold you. You will be the First Ladies of the Apocalypse, and we'll rebuild this world the way it always should have been. Then, together we will cast our Heavenly Father into the Void."

"We'll be truly free," I say, my warm breath hanging in the still night air. "The people of the future won't ever have to endure His tyranny. He'll become myth, no more than a children's fairytale."

"And our children will rule the New World while we reign in Hell. We'll make our own Eden, one where it is no sin to eat and fuck and enjoy the pleasures of the flesh."

"Speaking of..." I smile suggestively. "May I have you in this form, my King? All Hallows' Eve will soon come to an end, and I miss you already."

"You needn't ask, my beauty," he answers, dragging his thumb over my lower lip. "I'm more than happy to fill you with my seed at every given opportunity."

My cunt aches at his words. *God damn! Filled with the hot spunk of the Devil. Could there be any greater bliss?* "I'll be taking the lead on this one, Dark Lord," I insist, shoving him backward. Lucifer just grins, allowing himself to stumble back. He lands on his ass upon the colorful earth, and I pounce like a cat. I whip his pristine white robes aside to reveal the most beautifully angelic cock I've ever beheld. And it occurs to me that this'll be the fourth cock of Lucifer's I've seen. Fucking insane. There was his huge, thick, dark satyr beast, the red, double cocks of doom in his epic dark form, and now... I get *pretty angel dick!*

Mounting Lucifer, I slide his cock along my wet slit, guiding it salaciously down between my flaps, and to my hungry hole. I hiss through my teeth as I lower myself onto him, my thighs trembling with the effort after a night of constant sexual exertion. "Oh, my love," I moan, as I take him to the hilt, my cunt coming to rest against his firm, pink sack.

Lucifer takes hold of my hips, and lends me his strength, his lips slack with desire. "You feel like you were made for me." He growls.

I grin as I build my rhythm. "Maybe I was?" With my Fallen angel's help—and the last of my energy—I bounce, sliding up and down him for all I'm worth. "Oh, my fucking God!" I swear, eyes wide as new sensations ripple through me to tickle my raw clit. "Holy shit. Are you vibrating?" I gasp.

My sapphire-eyed angel smirks. "What can I say? I have a few tricks up my sleeve."

I pick up my pace, spurred on by the sheer gut-wrenching ecstasy assaulting me from within. I hurt, I'm tiring, and I honestly thought I wouldn't be able to feel for weeks after what I've been through tonight—but I was clearly wrong. *Who knew the body was capable of feeling so damn much?* I marvel. The lengths to which you can push it is both truly incredible and slightly frightening.

Moan after labored moan escapes me, and I lean forward, using the Devil's muscular chest for support.

"Lucifer, my love," I whisper. And then I guide his hands from my hips to my throat. "Choke me." The angel's eyes darken to the deepest shades of the ocean's mysterious depths, and he snarls, his grip tightening satisfyingly around my airway. As he holds me, I am at his mercy, on my whim. And I love it.

The shorter my breaths, the needier I feel. Horny doesn't even begin to describe it. The corners of my vision begin to darken, and I hear my own desperate rasps for air. I slam my cunt down on Lucifer with wild hunger, over and over again. I imagine that I'm a nice, tasty piece of rump, and that I'm impaling myself on a beautiful blade—one that carves me up just the way I like. Darkness closes in, and I moan, guttural, raw, and on the verge of a fucking titanic orgasm.

Seeing me struggle, Lucifer takes over. Easing his grip on my throat just enough to allow me to catch my breath, he raises his hips, topping me from below. He's like a literal jackhammer, and I can only utter a string of incoherent, garbled noise as he pounds my tender, spasming cunt into utter oblivion.

Chapter Nine

I'm alone tonight. The Wildes have accepted my decision with grace, and now my twin daughters, Amara and Layla, will guide the next generation of witches. No Wildes witch has ever chosen to leave before her time … but then, there's never been a witch made a Queen of Hell before. And after a long, and well-lived life full of memories, I'm finally ready to end my life on my own terms.

I could go on, I suppose. But I don't want to. I feel I have no more to offer my girls, my family, or this world. I want to step into the realm of the eternal and take my place beside my Master, my King, and my love, the one and only Lucifer Morningstar. After the better part of a century apart, I yearn for his touch more than the first blossoms of spring crave the heat of the sun. The feel of his fangs at my throat, the shadow of his great torn wings against the moonlight, and his beautiful sapphire eyes still haunt me all these years later.

With my affairs in order, I walk out into the forest behind my family home, following a path known only to me—to the very spot where the Devil claimed me as his bride when I was just twenty years old. A smile plays upon my lips as I trail my fingers over the rough bark of the trees, the cool soil shifting, and the colored leaves of Fall crunching underfoot.

My long silver hair whispers to my waist as I walk bare as the day I was born toward my destiny. A part of me wonders if I should be afraid, if I should fear the end, like so many of us have been taught to. Death is the dark terror and emptiness that swallows you whole when the thread of your life is cut short by his razor-sharp scythe. But the other part of me can only shake its head, filled with the certainty of hope, and the promise of an eternity beside the Fallen angel who took it upon himself to spare my ancestor, hundreds of years ago, today.

Arriving at our sacred clearing, where our sex and blood mingled with the earth, I put down my small satchel and mark my ceremonial circle. Despite the wrinkles that now mar my once youthful hands, it feels like just yesterday I lit these very same candles. The fragrance of their scented beeswax is familiar, and the soft glow of the flames flicker in defiance of the darkness of All Hallows' Eve. *And that's us*, I think to myself. *We are the little flames standing boldly in defiance of God's tyranny.* Pride fills my veins as I pick up my athame. I have no regrets. I'm ready to commit. I'm ready for the next frontier.

The candles blaze as I call out to my King, summoning him to Earth for the second time in my life. The wind picks up, howling through the trees, and the supermoon of All Hallows' Eve dims, darkened by wispy clouds that looks like silver-limned cobwebs stretched across the sky. In a breathless instant the forests of Salem fall unnaturally silent and my candles are extinguished, plunging me into darkness.

I grin. "A dramatic entrance indeed, my love," I say aloud to the night. The clouds above shift, dispersing into the atmosphere and the moon shines bright, illuminating the world once more. My breath hitches in my throat and tears prick at my eyes. Lucifer stands within my sacred circle, just as he did so many years ago—complete with cloven feet, gleaming black ringlets, and dark eyes that whisper of the secrets of eternity.

"I've missed you, wife," he says, stepping forward, muscles flexing in the moonlight.

Unable to hold them back, my tears spill, and my

smile wobbles. "I've missed you, too, husband." I sniffle, giddy with relief and joy.

"You look just as beautiful as I remember," he says, stroking my cheek with the backs of his fingers in that familiar way that still makes me weak at the knees.

"I'm old now, Lucifer." I laugh. "Silver hair, tired eyes, and sore bones."

"Are you?" he asks, his expression cheeky and his brow quizzical. "You look no different to me. I think perhaps your eyes betray you, my pretty."

I offer a wry smile in return for his flattery, but he gestures toward a seasonal puddle, and I approach it with curiosity. Leaning over to view my reflection in its mirror-like surface, a choked sob escapes me. "Oh, Master!" I touch my face, awed by my smooth skin, bright eyes, and brilliant blood-red hair.

Lucifer smiles. "Are you ready to go home, Mrs. Morningstar?"

****

I gasp in awe as we appear in what can only be the Great Hall of Hell. I glance behind us, and three grand thrones built entirely of bones and skulls stand tall, one large, flanked by two smaller ones which flirt with a slightly more feminine style. A great roar startles me, and I turn to face the hall. A sea of demons and Fallen angels, both grotesque and beautiful, cheer, fists upraised in tribute and celebration. Beside me, Lucifer squeezes my hand. "This is for you, Willow," he says. "They've all been waiting, just as I promised."

Speechless, my hand comes to rest against my heart, and I realize that I'm no longer nude. I'm clothed in what must be one of the most splendid and regal gothic gowns to have ever been dreamed into existence. An elegant boned corset of blood-red—to match my hair—pushes my full breasts up to their best advantage, creating damnably enviable cleavage. The skirts are full and perfect for twirling. While the entire outfit is overlaid with sheer layers of a fine black lace, identical to the fingerless, elbow-length gloves now adorning my arms. I feel every inch a queen.

The Devil raises his hand and perfect silence descends. "Tonight, we welcome the Second Queen of Hell, home. She will be known as Willow, the Red Queen."

Another riotous cheer nearly shakes the very foundations of Hell, and I feel my cheeks flush with heat.

"Sister," says a raven-haired beauty with sky-blue eyes that burn with the fires of rebellion. She wears a gown of purest midnight, and a black crown—the telltale Tear of God imbedded into the flesh just above her brow.

My heart hammers in my chest. She can surely be none other than... "Lilith," I whisper.

"I am," she answers with a smile. "And now we are sister-queens." She places a matching crown upon my head, only mine features thirteen scarlet jewels, while hers features glittering onyx jewels.

I accept the crown and embrace her warmly.

"Welcome home, Willow. It's good to finally meet you." With that, she steps back, taking her place on Satan's right-hand side.

"Let the festivities commence!" Lucifer announces, clapping twice. The Great Hall transforms into a luxurious demonic wonderland. A dark orchestra appears and begins to play, and epic chandeliers bearing thousands of black candles descend to light the floor. Lucifer turns to me. "A masquerade ball to celebrate our newest queen," he says, offering me his hand. As I place my hand in his, he transforms. No longer the satyr, but the beautiful Fallen angel. Dressed from head to toe in elegant black, his white wings are gone, replaced by dark feathered wings. They hang neatly folded at his back, adding to his majesty. "May I have this dance?"

Guiding me to the floor, the denizens of Hell part for us, and we dance. It seems like we're gliding, our feet scarcely grazing the gleaming floor. Lucifer's intense gaze stirs a riot in my soul, and the ease with which he moves dampens my inner thighs. Countless years have made him the perfect dark alpha. His every step is fluid, calculated, and effortless. Everything about him screams predator. *And he's mine.*

Unable to resist, heedless of gentry of the Dark Court watching, I wrap my arms around his neck and crush my lips to his, desperate to taste and savor him after so very long. Cheers resound, and a familiar she-demon's voice rises above the din.

"Fuck yeah, bitches! It's on!" shouts Lilith, her goblet raised, an expression of glee on her face.

The King grins, shaking his head as chaos descends all around us. "You've done it, now, Willow," he says with a wink.

"Holy shit," I breathe. The court becomes a boundless orgy. Fabric and masks fly. Howls, shrieks, and cries of delight fill the air. And as I stand within the protective circle of my Master's arms, I gawp at the spectacle I started.

"Now," says Lucifer, tapping an elegant black-lacquered nail to his lips. "Where were we?" The mischief of the Devil is bright in his eyes, and he steals my breath away as he traps my lips with his.

I've never felt so alive! "Defile me," I whisper against his soft lips. "Right here."

"Are you sure, Red Queen?"

I bite my lip, then grin. "Do I need to ask twice?"

"Never." Satan snarls, snaring my lips as he wrests his fly free. Reaching under my mountain of skirts, he picks me up and carries me with ease to a heavily burdened banquet table. Flinging the food and drink to the floor, he lays me down. Then, holding my legs in the air, he rubs his beautiful angel cock up and down my glistening slit before driving himself home to the hilt. I cry out in ecstasy at the feel of him. Hugging my thighs, with my knees over his shoulders, he thunders into me, vibrating all the while, just like he did in Salem.

As my first orgasm mounts, and my cries of pleasure ring out in the Great Hall of Hell, I can't help but laugh with manic glee as the Devil's hot seed fills me. This is, without doubt, the best Halloween of my life. Though, Lucifer and I have all of eternity to top it ... I, for one, can't wait to explore all of our dark and infernal desires, together!

The End

FAEDRA ROSE

TWISTED DESIRES

Loving Monsters, 4

Faedra Rose

Copyright © 2023

Chapter One

"Wow," I breathe as I paddle through the ancient sea caves of Devil's Island. The timeless red and gold rock formations are breathtakingly beautiful. Eroded by the intense surf of Lake Superior over millions of years, the caves are popular with kayakers and tourists from all over the world. I'm Wisconsin born and bred, yet I've never seen this stunning and dramatic spot for myself—until now. After falling out with my college friends, it seems the perfect place to explore, get drunk, and nurse my sorrows on Halloween.

Local legends say an evil spirit dwells here. The natives claim to have heard it howling and roaring on stormy nights. The thought has gooseflesh prickling up my arms as darkness descends and the winds pick up. The waters of Lake Superior start to get choppy. *Maybe this wasn't such a good idea*, I muse as my head buzzes with warmth. But a part of me loves fear. I revel in it. I always have.

The thrill of danger pumps me full of adrenaline, and I find myself squinting into the gloom, surreptitiously glancing about as if something might just rise from depths to fulfill my most twisted All Hallows' Eve fantasies.

Resting my double-ended paddle over my lap, I adjust my bright orange life vest and reach for my bottle of bourbon. I shudder after taking a deep slug of the amber alcohol as it burns down my throat. Doesn't taste great, but it gets the job done. After screwing the lid back on, I slide it back down alongside my legs and dip my paddle back into the water. *Do I have a death wish?* I wonder. What kind of sane person drunkenly kayaks through caves at night—alone?

"Well," I say aloud to no one in particular, emboldened by the relaxing hum in my veins. "If my fuckwit friends weren't such jerks, I wouldn't be here, now, would I?" No. I don't have a death wish. I just need an escape. Time to rage. Time to be reckless. Time to get the frustration out of my system. "I didn't fucking kiss Jett! He's just a friend." I inform the darkness. But it doesn't matter. Jessica believes what she heard from some tart on campus, instead ... even after ten stinking years of friendship. She didn't even give me the benefit of the doubt! She didn't even confront me or speak to me. She just turned everyone against me on a whim like a butt-hurt little bitch. *Ugh!*

We were supposed to go out tonight. We were going to trick-or-treat together, then kayak out to Devil's Island to get smashed and camp the night away. There was going to be a bonfire and everything. I've been looking forward to it for months. I love Halloween. It's my favorite holiday, so spending it with friends and getting wasted was going to be next level. I needed this. It was going to be epic.

Scowling, I slap the paddle down across my lap, again. My so-called friends obviously changed their plans at the very last minute—without notifying me—which means they really are done with me. I've been cut out of my own damn social circle like a bruise on an apple. And here I am bobbing about in the dark like an idiot out of pure spite.

There's no one in sight, not at this hour, in these conditions. Though I know a volunteer ranger mans the Devil's Island lighthouse. But whoever they are, they can't possibly see me—not down here. And they wouldn't expect anyone to be out on the water at Halloween, anyway. It's just me, the lake, and my misery. I sigh.

A strange, mournful sound echoes around me—sudden and unexpected. I stiffen, frozen in place, eyes wide. *What the actual fuck?* That doesn't sound like the surf and wind howling through sea caves… It sounds too poignant. The lamentation itself is rife with emotion. I can tangibly feel it. There is no way that it's just the elements of nature bouncing and echoing off each other. It's almost like someone or something is calling out. It sounds lonely, I realize. And somewhere deep down inside of me, the call resonates. The sound could have come from my own damn soul.

I take a steadying breath and try to remain calm, though my rational and educated mind races for an explanation. *It's just nature, Bethany*, I tell myself. *Just like the scientists say. There are no such things as evil spirits or creatures from the depths. You've let the ancient stories get to your head like a kid afraid of the monsters under the bed.* Despite my feeble efforts to rationalize the strange sound, my gut isn't fooled, not by a long shot. I know what I heard. It wasn't the bloody wind, and it certainly wasn't fucking human.

Swallowing my fear like a bitter pill, I make the only decision that makes any sense. I'm going to get out of here. This was a stupid idea. But I've lost my way, and I can't remember which direction I entered the cave system from. As quietly as I'm able I scrounge around my legs for a flashlight. Raising it at eye level, up by my shoulder, I press the button, illuminating the sea caves around me. Gold and red sediment glitters in the light's beam. It's breathtaking. Then something splashes nearby, painfully distinct from the sloshing of the surf against the smooth rock walls.

Lowering the beam to the water's surface, I nearly drop the flashlight altogether when I see something move, made visible by the light penetrating the rippling depths. Any precious shred of calm I had remaining evaporates, and I begin to hyperventilate, my heart racing for a finish line that doesn't exist. My arm trembles and I reach for my throat with my free hand. Panic begins to overwhelm me and suddenly I can't breathe. I try to draw breath, but it's like my throat has closed, restricting my airway almost entirely. My chest tightens and burns like fire. The darkness begins to close in all around me.

I feel the flashlight slip from my fingers, lost to the turbulent waters of Lake Superior forever. *I can't breathe!* I cry out in my mind. *Oh, God. I'm going to die.* The devastating realization slams into my chest with the weight of a sledgehammer, and I swoon, gasping in vain as my kayak topples over and oblivion claims me.

A heartbeat later and the shocking cold of Lake Superior embraces me from all sides, jolting me back to consciousness. Inverted, I can't get free. My legs are firmly stuck. *Fuck!* My curvy girl ass and chunky thighs are going to be the death of me. *For fuck's sake, you've got to be kidding me!* I wiggle and squirm, leveraging my weight against the sides of the kayak, all the while upside down. I pull and push, but it's no use.

This is it. Fear floods me all over again with a fresh wave of equilibrium destroying devastation. I'm going to drown! Someone's going to find my cold, fat, bloated, and lifeless corpse stuck in my kayak. My parents will be alerted, and I'll be just another drunken Halloween fatality on the news. My ex-friends will probably laugh when they hear it.

Just as I'm ready to give up and kiss my bombastic ass goodbye, I feel movement in the water around me. Something slick snakes its way around my waist, and in the chaotic darkness of the world below the surface, I make out two glowing yellow eyes. They stare back at me, unblinking and curious. Pure terror takes a dump on my fucking soul, and I open my mouth to scream. The lake rushes in, eager to quench the fire in my burning lungs.

Chapter Two

Like the unexpected suddenness of a balloon bursting, reality returns in an explosion of confronting awareness. My eyes fly wide as powerful blows strike me with pinpoint accuracy between the shoulder blades. My body convulses in response, and my lungs instinctively purge themselves of the lake. Water burbles and splutters from me in heaving gushes as I gasp for breath. There's rock beneath me and I'm out of the water. *How?* Mind racing, I try to raise myself up, to see where I am. The strength holding me up suddenly vanishes, retreating in a slither of tentacles and back into the murky depths.

I scoot backward until my spine is pressed flat against the wall of the small, smooth ledge. With my gaze trained firmly on the swirling waters, I shiver from head to toe, unable to control it. Several minutes pass as I sit on the precipice of indecision. Whatever it was … it saved me. It pulled me from my kayak, got me to this ledge safely, and then struck me on the back to expel the water so that I wouldn't drown. *If it wanted to eat me, it fucking would have*, I reason.

Once my breathing steadies to a degree, I lick my chapped lips and decide on my next move. And it's positively batshit insane. "Hello?" I call out, my voice trembling as my teeth chatter. I can't believe I'm doing this... "If you can understand me, thank you for saving me."

The water stirs several feet away and I squint, with only a shaft of moonlight pouring in through a crack above to see by. Long, wet black hair rises slowly from the water, followed by those glowing yellow eyes, and then the rest of a surprisingly handsome and chiseled human-looking face. Aside from the fact that the monster's skin is a deep shade of mottled orange, he'd almost pass for a man, features-wise at least.

I hold my breath, and we stare at one another for a handful of anxious heartbeats. "Can you speak?" I venture, when the silence hanging between us becomes unbearable.

The monster blinks two sets of eyelids, eliciting a gasp from me, before answering. "I can."

My mind reels as I run a hand through my tangled bleach-blonde hair. "What are you?" The monster rises higher, his entire torso—that of a man—breaks the surface. His muscles gleam as water cascades over his rippled form. Then tentacles appear. There's fucking eight of them! Some snake along the surface provocatively while others walk him along the cave floor.

"I am what I am," he says succinctly. "No more and no less."

His deep baritone washes over me, and to my shame I feel warmth blossom within me. It's the voice of a seasoned rock star, the type with that natural gravel that can make a girl lose her panties in a New York minute. I've officially lost my mind. Hot for a monster? Seriously?

"You look like a..." I pause, considering my words, but there really is no polite way of putting it. "Like a monster."

The monster smiles then, revealing sinister fangs. "Yes. I've heard that word before. Your kind lacks my beautiful appendages, so I suppose they might appear rather shocking to the unappreciative eye."

"Your tentacles?" I ask, dumbfounded. "Yeah, we humans don't have those."

"That's a shame for you," says the lake monster. "They really are quite useful."

Lost for words, the first thing that pops into my

head is what spills from my lips. "I can imagine."

His dark brows quirk, and he moves closer still. "Can you?" he asks, his voice dripping with salacious promise.

I blink, realizing what I've just fallen headlong into. *Oh, hell no!* "I, ah—I guess you don't get many visitors?" I ask lamely, attempting to deflect and diffuse the unnerving and increasing tension.

"No, I don't. You're the first in a very long while," he drawls, moving closer.

"Do you have a name?" I blurt, desperate to stall the monster's deliberately slow and predatory advance.

"I do."

Closer.

"What is it?"

"Why do you want to know?"

Closer.

I swallow the stubborn lump in my throat and feel my cheeks flush with an impossible heat. A tentacle slithers around my waist and I ignore it by sheer force of will. "Well, what am I supposed to call you, then?" I ask. "How do I thank you properly if I don't know your name?"

"I do not give my name lightly, pretty girl. For tonight, you may call me Master ... and I can think of other ways you might show your gratitude to me if you so desire."

My heart thrums in my ears as tentacles snake around my wrists, pulling my arms above my head. A gasp escapes me, and then the monster's lips are pressed to mine, his tongue snaking between them to explore my mouth. Despite the coldness of the lake, his kiss is surprisingly warm. His hands reach for my face, alighting softly on my cheeks, before trailing down my neck, to my sodden, see-through t-shirt to cup my ample breasts.

I break the kiss, trying in vain to pull back, but he holds me firm. There's nowhere to go. And there's nothing I can do. He has my arms secured, and a fore-tentacle wrapped firmly around my waist. "Wait," I breathe, breathless as a heady mixture of fear and curiosity dances through me. "What the hell do you think you're doing?"

"What does it feel like, pretty?" he drawls, tweaking my frozen nipples painfully with a wickedly suggestive smirk.

I yelp, then bite my lip. "I-I..." I stutter, starting over a handful of times, seemingly unable to get the words out. It's like I've lost my command of coherent speech. I scream internally in frustration.

"Let's keep this simple," the lake monster suggests. "How about I ask the questions, and you simply answer with *yes* or *no*?"

With no other option available to me, given my shameful and sudden tongue-tie, I nod warily.

"Wrong answer," he says, tweaking my nipples again.

A yip escapes me, and I fight to keep my breathing steady. "Yes," I gasp.

"Yes, what?" he presses, his glowing eyes holding my gaze.

Fucking Jesus! What the fuck am I supposed to do? *Play along.* The answer pops into my head unbidden. *It might be the only way to survive until morning...* Truthfully, I don't know shit about this monster. Is it benevolent? Or will it finish what the lake started when he's had his fun? I can't possibly know. But there's at least five damn hours until the sun rises and no chance of help whatsoever.

The only thing I can do is agree with my feminine instincts. They've helped countless generations of women survive the ages despite their abusers. So, I'll play his game and with any luck, tonight won't be my last.

With my resolve steeled and my heart set on survival, I take a deep breath. And though my voice quivers with fear, I give my answer. "Yes, Master."

Chapter Three

The monster's smirk would be enough to soak my panties—if they weren't already saturated with freezing-cold lake water. I shiver in his grasp as a tentacle snakes under my skirt, the transparent fabric sticking to my chunky thighs like a wrinkled second skin.

"That's a good girl," he praises as my legs spread of their own accord. "I may be a monster, but I know how to please a woman."

My brows furrow and I bite my lip, whimpering as his nubile appendage begins to play with my clit. Conflicted, I try to pull away, but in the same breath my body betrays me, and my hips lean into the monster's ravenous touch.

"Look at you. Your modest mind and childhood fears would have you withdraw and fight me. They would force you to deny your innermost twisted desires, but your primal soul craves me. I can see it, smell it … taste it," he finishes. He steals another kiss as the tentacle between my legs ramps up its wickedly delicious ministrations.

"Oh my God," I gasp against his mouth as I squirm on my ass against the smooth rock ledge.

"There is no god here but me, my pretty," he answers, nipping at my lower lip with his fangs.

Pain—though fleeting—registers as blood begins to bead from the small puncture wounds to trickle down my chin. It feels disturbingly and blessedly warm against my cold skin.

The monster licks the blood away, his eyes blazing. "Delicious." He draws another whimper from me with ease as the sensations below my navel change. It's as though he's sucking on my clit, though his face remains right here by mine, watching for my reaction.

"What is that?" I manage, my breathing growing heavier with each passing moment.

"What is what, pretty?" he drawls with malicious feigned innocence.

I bite back a moan as the intensity grows. "It's like ... like you're sucking on me."

"Ah, that. I have placed one of my suckers directly over your precious pearl. Do you like how it feels, or do you need more?"

My cheeks flare with heat, my nipples tingle—hard as rocks—and it feels like I'm perilously close to *something*. "Master," I whimper, unable to hide the sulk in my voice. "I've never felt anything like this before."

"You are no virgin," answers the monster. "I know it just by looking at you. There is confidence in your bearing. You know what it means to be with a man."

"I do," I gasp, squeezing my eyes shut tight. My insides contract, and my pussy quivers. It's like I can feel my heartbeat in my clit! When I open my eyes several desperate breaths later, the monster looks alarmingly disgusted, though his tentacle continues to pleasure me with effortless deviance.

"The men you've been with have taken their pleasure, and not given in return?"

I grimace against the intensity building within me, gasping aloud as his fingers brush over my sore nipples. "They've gone down on me," I admit in between breaths. "But it's never felt anything like this. I feel like I'm going to explode, or piss myself, or something! I don't know," I finish, overwhelmed with frustration.

"You've never come," says the monster with fire in his golden eyes. "Bastards." The amount of venom surprises me.

"I've always assumed I couldn't ... that there was

something wrong with me. I thought maybe I was just broken."

The monster shakes his head with a dark smile. "Oh no, precious girl. You can, indeed. I can hear your heart racing, your breath quickening. All the telltale signs are there, my beauty." I feel his sucker pull away, and instead he rubs my clit with the soft, but firm end of his tentacle, working it like a trigger on the battlefield. "Now, come for me," he commands, pushing me over the edge.

"Oh my G—" I bite off my blasphemy with a sharply drawn breath. "Master. It's happening. I can't..." My legs tense, my cold toes curl, and a strange keen that I scarcely recognize as my own voice escapes me. I can't help it. I can't control it. I can only feel, and bear witness as my body takes over, forcing my mind to take a back seat. There's nothing but fire and unrelenting ecstasy. My cunt spasms, and a warmth unlike any I've ever experienced before fills me, radiating from my pussy in pulsating, breath-stealing waves that consume me.

"Jesus Christ," I gasp when the intensity finally begins to wane, and I can feel my toes again.

"That was magnificent," says the monster, having drifted back a little way in the water to watch me, as if I were an actor on stage performing for a live audience.

"Magnificent?" I roll my eyes, fatigued. "I feel like I just died a million times over!"

"You just experienced your first release, pretty. From the lip bite to the scrunched brow, to the way you ground your ass against the stone in desperation, toes curled and white with strain—it was *magnificent*." Without having to ask or beg, the monster gently releases my wrists, and the tentacle that had been securing my waist withdraws silently back into the depths.

"Thank you," I whisper, as I attempt to get a little

more comfortable on the ledge in my soaking, disheveled state.

The lake monster quirks a dark brow, his expression stern. "Do you need to be punished, beautiful one?"

I gulp, pursing my lips in apology before I answer, almost forgetting the dangerous game I'm playing. "Thank you, Master."

"Better," he acknowledges. "But that's the second time now."

"I won't do it again, Master," I say, lowering my gaze to the dark, swirling waters.

"We'll see," he says.

A wave of exhaustion floors me in the wake of my near-drowning and first earth-shattering orgasm. "What now, Master?" I ask, rubbing my arms to fight the shivering cold prickling my skin.

"Tell me your name."

"It's Bethany Summers," I answer. "But everyone calls me Beth."

The lake monster slinks through the darkness like the perfect predator, and the dangerous glint in his eye has me backing up on the ledge. *Oh shit.* "I'm sorry, Master. Damn it. I'm not used to this. I've never even had a long-term boyfriend, let alone a master!" I explain.

"Well, Bethany Summers," drawls the monster, closing the distance between us once more. "That makes three. It seems you need a heavier reminder to watch your manners. A lesson, if you will—a heavier hand."

What does he mean? I wonder with sudden panic. *What's he going to do to me now?* There's nowhere for me to go. I'm trapped like a mouse in a dark, flooded maze.

The monster seizes my ankles with a pair of synchronized tentacles, pulling me forward so that I'm forced to lie on my back. Propped up on my elbows, fear races through me. Sinking deeper in the water until I can feel his hot breath on my cunt, he smiles as his fingers explore my folds. "I'm going to eat you until you cry, Bethany. And if you try to pull away or fight me, I'll only make it last longer. Understood?"

A mewling whimper slips from my lips as I try to relax. Prone, exposed, and helpless, I'm completely at his mercy. "Yes, Master," I whisper.

Chapter Four

Time loses all meaning as the tentacled lake monster chows down on me like I'm a fucking hot, crisp, soft, buttery, and sinfully sweet croissant fresh from the oven. I can't even think straight. It's like my cunt is a fucking puzzle box and he wrote the damn manual on it! My body shivers against the onslaught of conflicting sensations. Pleasure wars against the cold, lighting a fire within my belly to warm me, as the chill of my wet clothes and the breeze through the caves work together to steal every ounce of comfort from me.

The monster's tongue tickles my clit, before sinking inside of me. I let my head fall back against the time-worn rock, fighting the overwhelming urge to cry. A gasp rips from me as a sudden sting sings across the flesh of my ass, shocking me. I raise my head to meet his gaze, eyes welling with tears against my will.

"You're holding back," he accuses, his voice like rolling thunder. "Are you ready to let go?"

"No, Master," I answer, a surge of unexpected fire blazing to life within me.

"No? Look at that passion in your eyes, Bethany. It's captivating. You're willing to fight me on this, now, are you? You don't want to make my task easy?"

Emboldened by the flames burning inside of me, I hold his gaze with as much courage and defiance as I can muster. "Why should I, Master? You hold all the strings. I'm merely your waterlogged pleasure puppet."

"Oh, beautiful girl. You don't know what you're doing to me, do you?" he growls. "I can't resist a challenge. Do you truly desire to be broken? I could do it," he promises. "You aren't the first to have foolishly gotten lost in my lair. Or the first to have fallen prey to the Devil of Lake Superior."

A tentacle toys with my puckered asshole, teasing me open, before slowly—ever so slowly—slithering itself in.

"I've had much practice over the years. If you desire it, I could draw so much ecstasy from you that you'll wish for death's release. It would be a shame, in a way. You are the most voluptuous goddess to have tempted me."

"A wager, then," I gasp as his glowing yellow gaze bores into mine, and another tentacle pries its way inside my pussy. "Fuck," I moan, dragging out the *u* until I run out of breath.

The lake monster's eyes somehow gleam all the brighter. "What kind of wager, my pretty?" he coos too softly. The tentacles inside me begin to thrust, pumping me at alternating speeds like it's some kind of malicious team effort. "Are you sure you want to play this game with me? I must warn you. I've never lost a bet."

This isn't the meek and mild survive-the-night plan, I warn myself as his words drip over me. *This is playing with fire!* But within the dappled moonlit shadows of the Devil's Island caves, I feel compelled to follow the light inside of me that rages against the darkness. I might be a larger woman. And I might be most men's drunken mistake or second choice. But I am not a victim. Some ancient, angry, and defiant part of me refuses to be. It screams: *Break me! Do your worst. But I will not go quietly!*

My heart swells with the courage of every woman in history to have faced a monster and lived to tell the tale. Not because they took what was coming to them, but because they refused to be tamed. I will not just weather the storm. I will fucking ride the storm! As two more tentacles fiddle with my poor, oversensitive nipples, I grit my teeth. "I've never been surer, Master," I snarl.

"Color me intrigued, Bethany. State your terms."

The monster tries to scatter my wits, driving his meaty appendages deeper inside of me, pumping me in both holes with a maddening vengeance. Panting against the pleasure that would rob me of my rational mind, I flex my cold, white fingers against the stone, my short nails scraping against its time-worn surface. *What's something he has no control over? What's something I'm really fucking good at?* I rake my mind for options, scouring my brain for something—anything remotely viable—when it occurs to me. "If I can make you come with my mouth, you let me leave when the sun rises, alive and unharmed." I declare. If nothing else, I'm more than confident in my ability to blow a mean dick. A half-human-like monster's cock couldn't be that different, right? A man's a fucking man!

"And if I win?" he presses.

"State your terms, Master," I counter, feeling smug.

With his eerie glowing eyes focused on my face, he rubs his chin like an authentic villain deep in thought. "You are strong and brave, Bethany Summers. And I have no desire to end your life. But if you fail to make me come with that divine, pouty little mouth of yours, then you will remain here with me. You will be my mate, and together we will bring little tentacled devils into this world."

I hear his words as clearly as a clarion bell through the rapture assaulting my body. *Mother of monsters?* I want to respond, to fight, to do something! But in the next instant the monster descends upon me, tentacles still fucking and teasing my flesh in a cacophony of traumatic bliss that has me bucking and thrashing like a worm on a hook. A keening wail tries in vain to slip from my lips but is caught and silenced as he wraps me up in his arms and kisses me, his lips capturing mine with such feverish hunger and passion that it's the final straw.

Tears stream down my cheeks as I experience my second earth-shattering orgasm. It feels like my soul is being physically ripped from my goddamn body. I can feel everything and nothing all at once. My cunt spasms and contracts as wave after crippling tidal wave surges through me with tyrannical brutality, setting every single nerve ablaze, immolating me from within. The monster is inside me, on me, and all around me. His breath is mine, and mine is his.

To my deep shame I thrust against his hard form and vicious tentacles, desperate to eke out every ounce of ecstasy. It's like my body is my own worst enemy as it melts into the monster, allowing him access to the deepest, most sacred and virginal parts of me that exist— parts of me that will never be the same again.

And in the back of my mind, as I ride the breaking wave of paradoxical pleasure like a frenzied valkyrie, a dark thought emerges. *What if he's ruined me for all men? Even if I survive this, what if no man can hold a candle to the raging inferno of dark, tentacled devilry that is my monstrous master?* The very idea is deeply and disturbingly sobering.

Chapter Five

"When you're ready," says the monster, observing the mess of humanity that was once me lying in a languid pile, the waters of Lake Superior sloshing at the edges of my perch.

"I need a breather," I gasp. Despite the icy water, the whistling wind, and the cloying feel of my clothes against my damp skin, I'm no longer cold. Every inch of me thrums, alive and warm—but I'm so very tired. Tired doesn't even touch it. Not really. I feel like a wrung-out cloth, crumpled, used, wet, and in desperate need of at least a few hours in the sun.

"Do you wish to concede, Bethany?"

"And be your fucking monstrous baby mama?" I answer.

"Forgetting something?"

"Fuck you," I spit with a surprising amount of venom in response. I know exactly what he wants to hear. "You can stick your *Master* up where the sun don't shine!"

A dangerous gleam flashes in his eyes at my remark, and I brace myself for what's to come. A slap? A spanking? A brutal onslaught of nipple tweaks? Whatever the punishment, I can handle it. I must. I'm going to win this thing. I'm going to outplay the Devil of Lake Superior and start over. Fuck my useless friends, fuck the guys who treated me like a piece of meat … fuck them all. Including this cunt!

But the monster only smiles this time, and somehow, it's even more intimidating than punishment. It's a clear warning and a dark promise. "A fire has sparked within you, I see," he observes. "You know, you might just enjoy your time with me, Beth," he drawls. His long black hair spirals lank and wet over his strong shoulders, drawing my attention unwillingly to his rippling, muscular chest.

"I doubt it," I answer, infusing my words with all the snark I can muster.

"You have so far," he says leering, before a few of the monster's tentacles resurface, a bleached white skull in each of their curled grips.

My heart almost stills in my chest, and I forget how to breathe. The fire in me sputters, choking on its own smoke. There's no mistaking just what kind of skulls those are. They're human. Fuck me!

"Do you wish to join them, then? They chose not to enjoy my company," he remarks too casually, inspecting the remains with a cruel and bored curiosity. "This was Becca," he says, gesturing to one. "And that was Charlotte. And those two over there were men, I think. I want to say Luke and Martin?" He waves flippantly with sinister delight, clearly reveling in my unmasked horror.

"How did they die?" I whisper, my voice trembling with a newfound appreciation of the devil I'm dancing with. *Shit. Shit. Shit.*

The monster taps his chin with a single long orange finger, his eyes narrowing as if in thought. "Hm," he says. "I know I drowned at least one of them. She wouldn't stop screaming. It grew tiresome, so I just fucked her before she went cold. The other? I ate her. Her heart stopped beating at the mere sight of me, and I was hungry, so…" he trails off before continuing. "And the men? Well, one begged me to fuck him to death—that was delightfully messy—and the other went out swinging. But it makes little difference as to their fates. I always take what I want."

"You ate someone…" Every muscle in my body

locks up, the warmth of my relentless orgasm long since gone. I feel as cold as a corpse in the grave. I don't know what the fuck I was thinking. It would have been better to drown than end up here in the caves, playing at deals with such an unholy creature.

"I have," he answers. "Several someones over the course of my very long life, in fact."

"How old are you, exactly?" I ask. I wrap my arms around myself, my back to the stone as far as I can possibly go.

"It's hard to say, pretty. Several hundred of your years at least that I recall. I feasted upon darker-skinned humans—the natives of this land—long before your shade of white arrived upon its shores. And before that, islanders, when I still lived out at sea."

My mind is reduced to static, and I tangibly feel the blood draining from my face. "Is this wager a lie?" I grimace as my voice borders on plaintive. "Are you going to kill me no matter what I do?"

The monster frowns, folding his muscular arms across his chest. "No. I might be a monster, sweet thing, but you have my word. I have no desire to end your life. Too long have I been alone, and the one offspring I managed to sire has since traveled far from here. I desire new life, Bethany Summers. If you lose, your reward will be my heart, and an eternity by my side, here in the lake. Together we will spawn a family, and you'll have children to call your own. You will be a mother, and you'll never have to face losing them, for they will outlive both of us."

My teeth chatter as the reality of my predicament sinks in. "What do you mean?" I ask, eyes wide. "I'm going to change? Become like you?" The thought churns my stomach, and I hug myself protectively. *Tentacles? Me? No, thanks!* "You should have left me to drown in my kayak," I utter under my breath. "There is no hope for me, is there?"

"There is always hope, dear girl. I have waited centuries for a female strong enough, bold enough, and smart enough to carry my legacy into the future. Birthing a baby of my species is a trial in and of itself, you see. Only the strongest survive. And I know you will, Bethany. After centuries alone—after almost giving up on ever finding my match—destiny has delivered you to me. We are Fated Mates. You mightn't see it now, but you will feel it in your very bones soon enough, and then, you will never want to leave me, I promise you this. But I will keep my word, and I wish you luck in your impossible task."

Swallowing the dry lump in my throat with substantial effort, I purse my lips before asking my final question. "And how many women have you actually made pregnant if you've had just the one surviving child?" Awaiting his answer with bated breath, a tangible knot of fear and anxiety twists inside of me like tangled seaweed caught in a violent current.

"Don't be afraid, my pretty," he responds.

His words fall on deaf ears as the world fades around me and my focus narrows. "How many?" I press.

"Too many to recall."

Well, that's fucking fantastic, I reel. *The odds are clearly not in my fucking favor. Even if I don't die today, the chances are the bloody monster that grows in my womb will kill me later.*

"Will you concede, and join me, Bethany? Or must we continue with this charade and wager for your freedom?"

Flicking my wet hair over my shoulders with solemn determination, I meet the monster's yellow gaze. "I think I'll fight for my freedom, thanks," I answer as evenly as I'm able, though my very soul shakes with mounting dread. "I owe it to myself to try."

The Devil of Lake Superior inclines his head, eyes flashing in the filtered moonlight. "I can respect that," he says with surprising sincerity. Rising higher from the water on his many tentacles, he reaches down before me, parting an almost invisible seam in his mottled orange flesh with his fingers, just above where his writhing appendages begin.

A horrified gasp escapes me as he eases out the biggest, strangest cock I've ever seen from within. It stands to attention, gleaming in the starlight. Strange, thick purple veins throb around its length in an alienesque spiral formation—just inches from my face. "Dear God," I breathe.

Chapter Six

"Something the matter, pet?"

I blink at the monstrous dick that twitches before me. Its smooth head has a soft rosy blush which stands out against the brighter orange shade of his flesh, and the deep, dark purple of the glossy, pulsing veins that spiral around it like choking vines. This vile beast is so fucking long and thick that I have no idea how it could possibly fit inside my cunt, let alone my mouth! *Jesus Christ.* As the cold vise-grip of reality tightens its cruel fingers around my throat, I realize I've just fucked myself over, big time.

Suppressing a sigh, I lick my lips and kiss my freedom goodbye. There's literally no way I'm capable of taking enough of that in to do anything for it. Quite frankly, it's petrifying. It's a beast of its own fucking merit. Maybe if I had no damn teeth, I'd have a better chance of shoving at least some of it to the back of my throat. But I know straight up, just by looking at it, that that bitch of a cock is too much for me. Too much for any human gob. *Fuck.*

"Hm?" the monster prompts, raising an eyebrow in an all-too-knowing query.

"Just kill me," I say, cringing at the sickening defeat in my own voice.

"I will do no such thing. You are my prize."

"You knew," I say, my lower lip wobbling as I fight back tears. "You lied to me. You said there was hope, but there isn't any! Just look at that bloody thing."

The monster bristles, perturbed by my brash accusation. "The hope was never for your freedom, Bethany. The hope was mine—for me—that you would become my mate."

"Fuck this!" I rise to my feet on the wet rocky ledge and dive, leaping out as far as I can beyond the reach of his tentacles. For several breathless moments I'm free. I break the surface again, gasping down a lungful of cool air as I begin to power through the dark water with whatever strength I have left. An insane, futile glimmer of hope springs up, buoyed by my unhindered escape. Is he letting me go? Maybe he doesn't want a mate that doesn't want him in return. I mean, he could have stopped me if he wanted to.

The choppy waters of Lake Superior toss me about like a rag doll, and I must fight not to be pulled under into the swirling depths coursing through the subterranean cave system. Running on pure adrenaline, I soon find my reserves failing me. Fear isn't enough, and I'm reminded again that I'm an unfit buxom bitch. I'm no reed that can be carried safely away on the tide … I've got tits the size of watermelons, an ass that has its own postcode, and thick thighs for days. The fuckers might look bouncy and generous in spandex, but now they're just dragging me down and tiring me out. And I don't have enough energy to combat the wrath of the lake during a Halloween storm, and deal with a fucking monster.

Maybe if I wasn't still hungover, half-frozen, and jelly-legged from multiple orgasms, I'd stand a better chance. But I guess I'll never know, because in the next instant I feel the unmistakable grip of a tentacle ensnaring my ankle. I scream into the night in frustration. He's not giving up on me. He's never going to let me go! I can't even bloody drown myself because he'll save me, not because he's a great guy, but because he needs a nice chunky breeder to bring his little devils into the world. *Fuck! Fuck! Fuck!*

Another tentacle seizes me around the waist, and

I'm drawn backward through the rough water, thrashing like a worm on a hook, until I'm face-to-face with the Devil of the Lake once more. I cough up the water I've managed to breathe in, and glare at him through the darkness. "I fucking hate you," I spit. Drawing my arm back to slap his stupidly beautiful face, he catches my wrist with ease, as if he saw what I had planned a mile away. I flail in rage and frustration. "None of this is fair!" I scream.

The monster watches me as he holds me at waist height in the water, a look of amusement quirking his lips. "Life was never meant to be fair," he says. "And you did not hate me a short while ago, Bethany. In fact, I think I gave you more pleasure than you've ever known."

I fold my arms and look away, brooding as I'm held at arm's length like some kind of frenzied kitten that might hiss and scratch if he lets me get too close. The worst part is that he's not wrong. This tentacled, orange octopus bastard is a magician in the bedroom ... or should I say sea-cave? He expertly extracted more ecstasy from me than I ever dreamed possible. And one thing is for sure and fucking certain: he *has* ruined me for all men. How can I go back to ham-fisted fumbling, and two-minute quickies—where I get zero satisfaction— after this? It'd be like tasting ambrosia, then being forced to eat dirt for the rest of my life.

As my rage simmers down, I find myself wondering and questioning my own resolutions. Why am I so angry? Why do I want to escape so damn much? What do I have to go back to, anyway? Debt for a college diploma that I don't even enjoy? Friends who had no qualms throwing me away at the first given opportunity? Parents that I never see because they're workaholics? And I fucking know they're secretly ashamed of me. They are both slender and driven, whereas I'm an overemotional lost soul who eats her goddamned feelings.

They likely couldn't even care less if I just vanished. It'd probably be a relief for them. It's not like they'd even have to mourn. They'd still have my little sister, Suzy, after all. The bubbly, blonde, energetic, and skinny preteen cheer queen. What am I but their overweight mistake? I'm unwanted by my family, friends, and almost every man I've ever met. It's like I'm the butt of some cruel cosmic joke.

On the rare occasion some half-drunk sod hooks up with my needy, low self-esteemed ass, their mates laugh and make barking noises at us—as if I were nothing but a four-legged fat bitch, literally—and mockingly call their buddy a chubby-chaser.

Yet, my brain slams on the breaks so hard I get mental whiplash, and my mindset does a fucking radical roundhouse Chuck Norris style. Yet, this admittedly gorgeous lake monster literally desires me above all else. He wants me to bear his children. He wants to spend all the long years of his monstrous life span with me. And he wants to pleasure me and fuck me until I'm a blithering subhuman mess of woman...

Not to mention he did save me. I'm not his second choice, or only choice. He has the luxury of time. He could tear my fucking head off and skull-fuck me and not think twice about it. But instead, he says Fate has delivered me to him. He. Desires. Me. And ... sweet fucking hell! I think some twisted, dark, and unapologetically adventurous part of me desires him too. Maybe, just maybe, we are Fated.

"Fuck me," I breathe as my gaze snaps up to meet his. Sudden clarity washes over me like the butt-fucking cold waves of Lake Superior.

"Is that an option, pet?"

Chapter Seven

This man—this male—this monster is my chance to start over and have a new life. Together, we can build our own family, just like he said—one that would last almost forever. We'd have each other, always. Until the end. And no one would ever shun me or hurt me again. "Yes," I say suddenly, surprising even myself as a small smile plays upon my lips.

"Truly, little wench?" he asks, clearly suspecting a ploy or trick.

I don't blame him, I think to myself. *I did just have an epic meltdown and tried to escape.*

"Yes," I repeat. "But there are conditions."

The lake monster quirks his brows and a deviant grin splits his face. "Name them," he says, his gaze hungry.

"There are three," I warn. "First, I want to know your name, because I'm sure as hell not calling you Master all the time. It should be saved for sexy times," I reason.

A growl escapes the monster's throat, and the tentacle around my waist tightens ever so slightly. "A name is a sacred thing. I haven't shared mine with anyone but my son, not even the other women," he answers. "To know a monster's name gives you power over them—the ability to summon them and control them."

I purse my lips. That checks out. Even in mythology and traditional lore, I know it to be true. The fae never share their full names for similar reasons, and when it comes to summoning monsters? Well, I think bloody mirrors, repeated names, dripping hooks, and fucking bees. I suppress a shudder. "If I'm to be your

Fated Mate, shouldn't I know it?"

"My—" he cuts himself off, his gaze glittering with an inner fire beneath the cold moonlight. "Don't play with me, pretty. What are you saying?" He draws me nearer, wrapping my thighs in another tentacle so that my weight is distributed more evenly, and I'm instantly more comfortable.

"I've spent my whole life for as long as I can remember hating myself. I've always been the curvy girl that gets too much attention—and not the good type. I've been the butt of jokes, I've been taunted, ignored, and made to feel worthless and ugly. And I've wanted to kill myself more times than I can count because of it." I pause, biting my lower lip for a moment before continuing. "But you think I'm worthwhile. You actually want me *as I am*. And I've never been wanted by anyone ever, not really." I lick my lips, shivering in cool night air. "And I want to be wanted."

The monster smiles, tilting his head as if in contemplation before answering. "My name is Kanaloa," he says. "And I am one of the kraken—half-man and half-octopus. Though your kind have called us gods of water and sea in centuries past. We have existed in these parts, around this land you call America, for time beyond memory."

"Kanaloa," I repeat. "It's beautiful."

"And your second condition, pet?" he asks.

"I want to know what will happen to me when I bear your child," I say.

"Once your body accepts my venom, you will change."

I scrunch my nose at the thought of being bitten. "I'll become one you? A kraken? Half-woman, half-octopus?"

Kanaloa laughs at my reaction. "You will, yes."

"Will it hurt?"

My would-be mate bites his lip and nods. "The power in my blood is an ancient one, Bethany. I have heard talk of your popular witches and wizards, and the magic they command. This is not like that. Blood magic is pain. Your limbs will break and split, the bones in your legs will shatter and be no more. And as your body remolds into its new form there will be an agony unlike any you have ever known. My first mate screamed until not even the magic in my blood could heal the damage done. She was mute from then on, until the day she died, which wasn't long after," he adds.

I tangibly feel the color drain from my face. "But If I survive the change, I'll be able to breathe underwater and swim wherever I want?"

"Your lungs will adapt, though you would not know it to look at you. You'll be able to breathe air and water, as I do. Even salt water, when we venture out into the great seas once more—where my great kind originated."

"And my third condition ... I need your promise, your oath. I want you to swear that you will never leave me. If I do this, if I throw myself in the deep end like this, I want to know that I'll never be alone again. And no other women!" I add as a jealous afterthought. "If I'm yours, you are mine—completely."

Kanaloa draws me near, until my soft, shivering body is pressed to his muscular orange form. "You have my heart's promise and my solemn oath that I will be with you always. I will never forsake you, and I will never be with another."

I search his eyes and I see no lies hidden there, only a starving and honest truth. His words move me, and a perfectly macabre serenity envelops me like the blanket of a starry night. And for the first time in as long as I can remember, I feel at peace. It's a strange and foreign sensation. The cold suddenly feels less intense, and my heart calms, ceasing its frantic thundering for a more even gallop.

Taking a deep breath, I reach out and touch his face as lightning cracks through the sky above. "Then what I'm saying is, I want to be with you, Kana," I say, my lips brushing his. "I accept Fate's call. I will be your mate."

My kraken mate wraps me in his tentacles, shielding my body from the storm with his own, then his mouth opens to me, and we share the most intense and passion-defining kiss of my life. The wind howls, kicking up the lake around us, and the clouds rumble as flashes of white-hot light streaks through the glittering heavens.

It's a picture-perfect moment, and one I doubt I'll ever forget. In the deep, treacherous waters of Lake Superior, there's just me and my monster. My Kanaloa. And nothing has ever felt more right, or wrong—and honestly, I'm down for both, because at this point … fuck it! Right?

Chapter Eight

Kana powers through the lake as I cling to his back for dear life, arms wrapped around his neck and legs about his waist. I shriek with excitement—the way you do on amusement park rides—just for the sheer thrill of it, but my voice is drowned out by the back-to-back claps of thunder. I've never felt more alive! My fear has evaporated like dew with morning's first light, and all that remains in its place is an unbridled and wild sense of freedom.

Before long, we find ourselves in a secluded nook of the lake, a little pocket bay shadowed from all sides by sheer rock faces. The water sloshes upon a small beach that leads up into the lush forest.

When I'm sure I can stand, I slide from Kana's back. It's surprisingly comforting to feel the sand between my toes once more. I smile as he reaches for my face.

"You will not have your legs much longer, mate," he says almost apologetically. "I thought you might like to stretch them and feel the earth beneath your feet one last time before your change."

I'm genuinely touched by his sincerity and thoughtfulness as I lean into his hand. Withdrawing, I trudge through the shallow water and onto the beach. The sand is cool and gritty, and I'm suddenly very, very aware of my weight. I glance down at my curvaceous form and grimace. Though I didn't notice at the time, the water offered me buoyancy. On land again, my voluptuous form feels strange to me—like I'm wearing extra layers that don't belong. It doesn't feel right. *I don't like it.*

"What bothers you, mate?" calls Kana, his many

tentacles moving him further up the sand toward me.

"It's just gravity." I sigh. "I'm not a fan, I've decided. I've honestly never spent so long in the water before tonight, and now ... it feels uncomfortable to be without it. I appreciate the thought, but I don't think I'll miss solid ground as much as you might imagine."

Kana extends his arm, offering his hand to me with a smile that says more than words ever could. "Come back to me, then, my beautiful Bethany. Let us consummate our union here in the shallows where the water is kind."

How could I have ever been afraid of this monster? I wonder. Everything about the kraken calls to me. There is nothing but lust and warmth emanating from him—no threat, but the promise of carnal intimacy and an eternity of deep, twisted pleasure.

I wade out to him, and he turns me around to face the forest.

"On your knees, Mate," he coaxes, his breath hot against my ear. "I want to see this big, white ass as I fuck you and claim you."

A shiver of excitement ripples through me. Wriggling out of my soaked skirt and t-shirt, I toss them onto the sand, bare as the day I was born beneath the brilliant All Hallows' Eve moon. Then without a word, I obey, dropping to my knees in the lapping surf. The water cradles my body as just my shoulders and the globes of my ass breach its surface.

"Beautiful," Kana whispers in his knee-weakening gravel. "I think I'm going to have to fuck it, too, once I'm done burying my seed deep inside your fertile cunt."

I whimper at the thought. *That huge thing up my bunghole? Jesus fucking Christ!*

"Good girl," Kana soothes, massaging his hands

over my thick cheeks before giving one of them a sharp smack. "Come now. Spread your legs just a little wider. That's it."

In the next instant he's sliding the rosy head of his monstrous cock up and down my bare pussy lips, smearing his slick pre-cum with long, languid strokes, teasing me.

"Master," I plead, glancing back over my shoulder, overwhelmed by my need to be filled with him. "I want you."

"It's been a long night," he agrees, dipping his enormous cockhead just inside of me.

I push back instinctively, desperate, wanting to bury that terrifying beast of a cock to the hilt, but his hand rests firmly on my lower spine, holding me in place.

"No, no, my pet," he says, clucking his tongue. "I will claim you when I'm ready, and not a moment before."

I bite my lower lip in frustration, and moan as a tentacle snakes around my thigh and between my legs to play with my throbbing clit. Two more tentacles caress my breasts and toy with my hard, oversensitive nipples. The pleasure is an exquisite agony, the warmth of my desire warring with the cold of the lake. But if I'm shivering, I don't notice. There's just my monster, me, and my fingers and toes digging into the silty sand.

It feels primal and wild to be on my knees like a bitch in heat, but it's not far from the truth. Kanaloa will be my master, my lover, my mate, and the father of my children … and I'll be his pet, his queen, his mate, and the mother of his children in return. Our union is one of lust and mutual benefit. We are two souls who have been alone all our lives, lost in a world that has no room for outcasts and rejects like us. Yet here we are, entangled and twisted, brought together by Fate itself. And in this beautiful, monstrous, and pivotal moment I want this kraken inside me more than I need air.

"Are you ready to be broken, Bethany?" asks Kanaloa, interrupting my heated reverie.

A hiss of desire whispers past my teeth. "Yes. *Please!*" I beg. I've never been more ready. A second later and a sucker captures my clit, pulsating with a vengeance. My legs shake, my heart races, and I grasp desperately at fistfuls of silt as my kraken plunges his huge, rippled cock into my wet and shuddering pussy.

A cry rips from my throat, echoing into the night, and my entire world narrows down to my poor, flaming cunt. The burning stretch as my body valiantly tries to accommodate his otherworldly dick consumes me, and then a tentacle wraps itself around my throat…

Chapter Nine

God, yes! The tentacle tightens its grip just enough to have me rasping for breath, but not choking. It's so fucking hot. My life is literally in my monster's hands, and it's erotic beyond measure. I push back, rocking my hips as Kana thrusts with long deep strokes. The ribbing of his spiraling purple veins heightens my ecstasy, and it's not long before I can scarcely hold myself up. Thankfully my kraken has got me. His pleasure-seeking tentacles work their wicked ways while ensuring my face stays above water.

Kana pounds me for all I'm worth, burying himself up to his hefty orange sac again and again, until I'm a blithering, gasping, moaning mess. His tentacles deftly bring me to climax—twice—before we come together. He unleashes his load, filling me like a baker piping a donut full of fresh cream.

I shudder in the wake of my brutal orgasms, shaken to my very core. If I have arms or legs, I can't feel them. Not anymore. I might as well be a bloody jellyfish. Every single inch of me is loose, relaxed, and like putty in Kanaloa's hands. Just when I think the violent fucking is over with, he withdraws and presses his cock to my asshole.

"Kana!" I squeak. Instinctively, my body tries to tense up, but it's like his seed has relaxed me somehow.

"Hush, pet," says my mate. "You are mine now. But before you become like me, I need to plunder this gorgeous ass."

My mind races, even though my body feels as dozy and blissed out as a kitten with a belly full of warm milk. Cunts are made for cocks … but asses? I cringe internally. *And he's so big!*

Kana smacks each globe of my ample ass, sending shock waves through me.

"I might die," I moan.

"You might wish for death, my beauty, but this will not kill you. Though you might never have known it, you were made for me. You need me the way I need you—completely."

Then my master sinks his ridged cock slowly inside of me. My ass caves for him, offering little resistance, allowing him deeper and deeper access, until I feel his firm body and smooth sac flush against me. It doesn't hurt anymore, shockingly. None of it does. Whatever magic Kana's cum has in it, it's reduced me to a paralytic fuck sock. And boy, does he take advantage of the opportunity! He reams me out, fucking me like a true monster. As if I were his supernatural equal and not just a small, curvy human woman.

Closing my eyes, I just feel. It's all I can do. The delicious assault goes on, his tentacles effortlessly finding my clit again. Between the great beast in my ass, and the sucker between my legs, the spankings are more than I can bear. As his hands paddle my ample cheeks, the sting reverberates through me. I can't even imagine how it must look—my butt must be as bright red as a beetroot beneath the moonlight as it's punished repeatedly for the sin of being too damn voluptuous.

In the blink of an eye, I'm lifted from the water and spun around to face him. He wraps his arms around me, holding me tight, his face buried against my neck as he reaches his release. Like a puppet in his embrace, I can only rest against him as he shudders and bucks, emptying his cum inside me. *We're done*, I think to myself with a small sigh of relief. I'm fucking exhausted! I need sleep. I need rest. But I'm wrong. This is only the beginning.

I gasp as Kanaloa's fangs pierce my neck, sinking

into my throat without remorse. He holds me in a viselike grip, and there's no escape. *This is it.* He's turning me— injecting me with his kraken venom. I might have liked some warning, but then, maybe this is for the best. And what does it matter? My mind is made up. I'm filled with his cum, and I'm going to birth his offspring. Pretense seems redundant at this point. There's just one last step to take on this wild journey, and he's thrown me in the deep end. I might as well learn to swim with the big fish.

His venom sears through my veins, burning like liquid wildfire. I want to scream, to writhe, and cry, but I can't. I'm paralyzed and my agony is mine to bear witness to alone. Like a rag doll I hang limp in his grasp, motionless, but inside I feel everything. I can feel the change taking hold, molding me into something new and monstrous. I hear the resounding snap of my legs breaking before I feel it. *Fucking Christ!* And from then on there is no coherent thought. There is just agony upon agony, laced with anguish, pain, and an uncanny, fathomless terror.

It goes on forever. Or at least it seems to. How much time truly passes, I don't know. But at some point, lucidity returns, slowly at first, like a flower shyly unfurling its petals to the dawn. Then the yawning maw of the void peels away, and I'm awake and finally aware.

The stars twinkle above like diamonds in the soft velvet twilight before sunrise, and I take my first breath as a kraken. I bristle, feeling sand beneath me. The beautiful orange-hued face of my mate comes into sharp focus, and I sigh.

"All is well, Bethany, my love," he croons, bringing his lips to mine in an intimate kiss.

When he withdraws, I raise myself up and glance down. I have eight fucking damn tentacles. "It's really me," I whisper. Reaching my hand out to explore my unique form, one of my tentacles curls up out of the water in answer to my will. "I don't understand," I say, my brows creasing. "You said that one of your other women screamed herself mute, but I couldn't scream even if I wanted to. I was trapped inside myself—paralyzed. I couldn't move an inch. It was..." I pause as flashes of my transformation play back in my mind, "a nightmare."

"Forgive me, pet. I learned after the first few hundred failures that changing my potential mates first was a gruesome mistake. The transformation is far too brutal to be endured by a human while conscious and physically aware. When I discovered that my cum has a numbing, sedative effect on women—no doubt nature's way of ensuring successful mating—I took advantage of the knowledge. I filled you with as much of my seed as I could before giving you my venom. I had hoped to spare you as much pain as possible."

Licking my lips, I offer my mate a sheepish smile. "Thank you. I don't think becoming a monster is an easy thing no matter how it's done," I say. "But if you prevented me from hurting myself, count me grateful. I'm just glad it's over."

"Your transformation may be, pet, but our adventure together has just begun. You are a newborn, and there is much to learn. You must learn to hunt and memorize the lay of the lake. I will teach you how to avoid being seen, and how to defend yourself if you ever encounter hostility."

"And how to fuck like a kraken, right?" I ask cheekily, running my hands over my full, naked breasts, and soft orange belly.

"That too," says Kana with a devilish grin, trailing his fingers over a sensitive spot a few inches below my navel. I shiver at his touch, gasping as his mouth catches mine. He slips two fingers into my hidden slit, revealing the location of my cunt on my newly changed body.

Without further prompting I kiss him back, hungry for more. Wrapping him up in my arms and tentacles, I allow myself to give in to my carnal needs. Then, together in the shimmering waters of Lake Superior, by the dying moonlight of All Hallows' Eve, we explore our most depraved and twisted desires.

The End

FAEDRA ROSE

LUNATIC DESIRES

Loving Monsters, 5

Faedra Rose

Copyright © 2023

Chapter One

The darkness beneath the trees is fluid, leaking between the gnarled and twisted trunks of the forest like spilled ink. It shifts with the wind as it howls through the night—almost like it's alive and stalking me—as I follow the well-trodden path toward Blackwater Falls. The shadows dance and sway, seemingly avoiding the moonlight's touch as it filters through the canopy in fragile shafts of glittering radiance. The moon hangs in the sky high above the world like a brilliant silver pendulum or a white-hot jewel.

It's All Hallows' Eve and it's a picture-perfect fall night, which suits my purpose perfectly. Readjusting my bag on my shoulders, I can't help the easy smile that creeps to my lips. Tonight, I hope to capture a truly breathtaking shot of the full moon hanging over the iconic falls. And if my photograph wins first place in the prestigious Western Viriginia Photography Awards, the five-thousand-dollar cash prize will be mine! It's enough to start over. *Just.*

I'll be able to afford a reliable car for the road trip and a few weeks' rent up-front when I arrive in New Orleans. I might have to find work along the way because nothing burns coin like gas … but to get out of here, I'd do anything.

Point Pleasant might be where I was born, but it's not where I'll die. My parents never made it out of this fucking State, but I will. I must. This place haunts me, and I can't stand it, and I won't. I refuse. Not for any longer than I absolutely have to.

Once I reach Louisiana, I can live the life I've always wanted. I can try and make a living from my art, make a real business of it. And life doesn't get more thriving, colorful, or interesting than it does in the old French Quarter. It's where I want to be, and that's why I'm here trekking to Blackwater Falls on Halloween. This is my chance and I'm going to seize it like a lifeline with both hands.

Hugging myself against the chill, I continue through the dark, until something unusual and unexpected catches my eye. I stop and do a double take, squinting through the shadows to make sense of what I'm seeing. *What the fuck?* It's … a locket—a real silver locket glittering beneath transient moonbeams. Approaching the branch from which it's dangling, I inspect the trinket by what limited, dappled light there is. It's beautiful and ornate but tarnished heavily by time and the elements.

Taking the locket in my hands, I trace my fingers over its surface, admiring its delicate heart shape and the floral filigree decorating its surface. "What are you doing here?" I ask aloud, my brows furrowing in thought. Is it lost or stolen property? *Who would leave such a timeless treasure hanging from a tree exposed to the weather?* Reaching for my phone, I wrangle it one-handed, turning on the light to better inspect the trinket.

With hesitant, careful fingers I open the heart to find a tiny, sepia-stained photograph of a man. Tilting my head, my curiosity aroused, I peer at the photo as my eyes adjust to the light. The man is handsome as far as I can tell, with a strong jaw, a serious expression, and short, slicked-back hair. He seems like a gentleman of a bygone era. Being sepia, and judging by the silversmithing of the locket, it must have been taken some time in the late 1800s. *This is a fucking heirloom! A piece of history*, I marvel.

Depending on who this man is, this could be worth a fortune. The jewelry alone makes it a timeless antique that deserves to be locked behind glass in a museum. So, what the hell is it doing hanging from a tree? Surely if this were hanging here earlier, during the day, some opportunistic bastard would have stolen it...

Which can only mean that someone hung it out here tonight. But I haven't encountered another living soul. The trail through Blackwater Falls State Park is dead silent, devoid of everything but the sounds of nature. I don't imagine anyone in their right mind would venture out here after dark. Especially not on Halloween.

Most folk in Point Pleasant are heavily superstitious, though they'd never admit it in this day and age. The cryptid icon of Western Virginia supposedly calls this town home—the elusive and terrifying Mothman of legend. First spotted in 1966, the rumors and sightings have circulated ever since. We even have an artistic metal statue of the monster on Main Street. It's a bit of a draw card when it comes to tourism for the area.

Don't get me wrong, I'm a fan of monsters. They're cool. They make for great horror movies and fun fiction, but anyone with a brain knows that shit isn't real. There's no God, no Devil, and certainly no fucking

Mothman. Obviously. Pursing my lips, I can't bring myself to leave the locket. There's no guarantee that someone with less honorable intentions won't take it in the morning.

At least if I take it, I can protect it until I'm able to get it valued and investigated. It might belong to a family that still lives in town. *Maybe I could reunite them with their precious heirloom! I imagine there's quite a story behind it.* I slip it carefully over the ends of the branch and secure it around my own neck for safekeeping until I get home. If it's around my neck, I can't lose it in the dark.

With a smile at my find, I move to step forward, only for my brows to scrunch again. I hadn't noticed at first, but there's a small trail that leads off the well-worn path by the tree from which the locket was hanging. *Curious. I wonder where it leads?* Being a bit of a "curiosity killed the cat" type, my heart leaps with excitement at the prospect of adventure. Judging from the direction it disappears into the forest, it just may lead to a lesser-known vantage point above the falls. And that idea has potential.

I won't be the first photographer to capture a nice shot of Blackwater Falls, but maybe I'll be able to snap an angle that hasn't been seen before. Perhaps that's what will help me secure a win—a unique view of one of the most popular tourist attractions in our State. Before I even consciously decide, I know I'm sold. The temptation is too great. The moon is bright, I have all my equipment, and a blazing hope for a new beginning. It's all I need.

Maybe this is Fate?

Sucking a deep breath into my lungs—the promise of a better future ahead of me—I glance down at the locket hanging between my breasts and set off down the obscure trail and into the night.

Chapter Two

The trail is narrow, and damp shrubbery brushes against my shoulders as I pass. I feel the moisture soak into my thin leggings as I go but shrug it off. What's a little discomfort for a chance to start over? The path winds this way and that, meandering in an odd pattern that slowly follows the incline of the mountain.

An owl flusters and hoots nearby, perhaps offended by my trespassing so close to her nest.

"I'm just passing through," I say, spying her magnificent golden orbs in the darkness of the treetops. "Never mind me." A smile quirks my lips as I move on. I can't imagine how wonderful the freedom of having wings must be. Flying anywhere you want, whenever you want—with nothing and no one to stop you! It must be marvelous. If I had wings, I'd leave this place and soar high above the world, skimming clouds and dancing with the wind.

A sigh escapes me, and I forge ahead, readjusting the straps of my camera bag. The night fills me with a sense of wonder. I may not be superstitious, but I love Halloween. It's a great holiday. Fall is one of my favorite times of year, and the decorations and festivities fit my Gothic style to a *T*. All I need to see are a few bats silhouetted against the brilliance of the moon, or the Mothman, and my All Hallows' Eve will be perfect.

The wind begins to pick up and I regret not grabbing my scarf on the way out as the chill breeze raises the tiny hairs on the back of my neck. I shiver involuntarily. The evening is satisfyingly crisp, but with the added wind chill it's definitely cold. It feels like it's going right through me, like a ghost transcending my flesh to steal all the warmth from my soul. *Come on,*

Penny, I chastise myself. *Ghosts? Really. As if!*

Time loses all meaning as I trudge on. The twisting, secret path seems to have no end. But it does end—eventually. My breath catches in my throat, my stomach drops, and my legs turn to jelly at the sight before me. A yawning maw of pitch-black darkness rears out of the earth like a pit of despair, swallowing all natural light that dares enter.

"Whoa." Every instinct screams at me that this was a mistake. My gut warms me to turn back and find an alternate route to the Falls, but another part of me yearns to risk life and limb for the sake of adventure. Where could it go? Why is it here? I can only guess. I'm alone and cell reception out here is sketchy at best. I'd be mad to go in. I stand at the cave entrance, dangling upon the precipice of indecision.

What if I fall? What if I damage or lose my camera equipment? I don't know where this hole leads, and if something happened to me, how long would it be until someone raised the alarm? How long until they began their search? Would they find me? I told no one where I was headed tonight. *There was no one to tell.* I grimace. With my parents gone, I'm practically alone in this world. I've grown used to being independent and making ends meet all on my own.

It's just me, myself, and I. If I don't make my dreams a reality, I'll end up stuck here, forced to endure a monotonous and unfulfilling life of shift work at the Seven Eleven in town. The thought gives me pause. I don't have insurance. If I get hurt there's no one to take care of me, either. But despite every rational and logical reason to walk away and never look back, I find my feet taking steps forward, toward the impenetrable, inky gloom.

Maybe I can explore just a little way in? A peek

couldn't hurt, could it? A distant voice on the wind calls out, or is it a bird screeching? Or perhaps my mind is playing tricks on me as nerves get the better of me. *There's no one here*, I assure myself. *Stop being a baby. It's just a peek!* Steeling my nerves, I shrug off my bag and leave it by the cave mouth. It'll be safer here, and I'll be more sure-footed if I'm unburdened. Checking my phone battery, my signal plunges to zero.

"Just a peek," I whisper. Raising my phone before me to light the way, I glance over my shoulder at the picturesque night once more, then step into the darkness. The ground beneath my feet is strangely smooth, as if worn down by feet over a long passage of time. Strange. The rest of the area surrounding the cave looks wild and untouched. Aside from the narrow path, there's no sign that this route is frequented by more than the odd explorer. It's too overgrown—too hidden. *Weird.*

Undeterred, I walk on, descending into the bowels of the earth and toward the unknown. Maybe, if Fate is kind and luck is on my side, this cave will lead me somewhere spectacular ... to a part of the Blackwater Falls never seen before! If it does, I can always retrace my steps and collect my equipment.

The path leads down, the darkness all-encompassing. It's cold, but without the breeze it's infinitely more bearable, and the deeper I venture, the warmer it seems to get. Makes sense, I reason. Bears like caves because they're safe and warm. *Bears.* "Shit," I breathe, my eyes widening in the gloom. I'm a fucking idiot!

Chapter Three

Holy crap. *Shit. Shit. Shit.* I'm unarmed and who knows how deep and far into this tunnel. But surely, if there were bears, I would have come across them already, wouldn't I? Heart racing, I feel torn. Go back while the going's good and get a damn shot of the Falls? Or explore on and find out just where this bizarre, smooth passageway goes? My inner rebel takes my fear and beats it to death before it can take ahold and destroy my Halloween adventure.

I've come this far without incident—I might as well go on. Soon the cave seems to bottom out and widen into a larger cavern. My phone light isn't powerful enough to see further than a few feet, but there's space all around me now, and I can no longer reach the cold, stone walls. "You're okay," I whisper. "Just keep the light ahead and watch your feet."

A deep and rumbling growl fills my ears and my heart bunny-hops in my chest. I can almost feel my life leave my body. *Oh no. Dear God, No!* I freeze as still as a statue, my phone still grasped firmly in hand. Every muscle in my body quakes with terror. I'm fucked. I'm so very, very fucked! I'm going to get mauled, eaten, and shit out by a fucking black bear! What a way to go. *Seriously. Fuck my life.*

So much for my new beginning. I'm going to die here in West Virginia, just like my parents, and I'll never see New Orleans. I'll never take another photo again. This is my curtain call. I hear the distinct sound of heavy footfalls on the earth, and in a sheer moment of panic I lumber backward. Something crunches horrifically underfoot, and I stumble right onto my ass. A shriek escapes me as I fall and it's amplified by the cavern, echoing in a mockery of my ungracious stumble.

I scramble backward and raise my phone before me like a shield of light. There're bones scattered all over the ground. Lots and lots of bones. And that cracking sound? A skull of some description that I just crushed with my boot. In the shadows beyond the reach of my pitiful light, I see a great lumbering shape. There is no mistaking the territorial huffing and low rumble of the bear as it ambles forward, closing in for the kill.

This is it. This is how I die. The bear draws nearer. It's so close I smell its breath now. There's nowhere to go. I can't outrun a bear. For a split-second I contemplate grabbing a broken bone and attempting to defend myself, but this beast is massive, and I just waltzed into its home. It's pissed. Even if I managed the odd stab or two, it'd be like tossing stones into the Grand Canyon. It probably wouldn't even feel it and then it'd gore my throat anyway.

It roars suddenly and its spittle flies at my face, its rancid breath blows my hair over my shoulder. I can't prevent the strangled scream that tears forth from my throat as I realize the bear's mouth is wide enough to just bite my face off.

A bloodcurdling screech vibrates through my soul, ricocheting off the rock walls to bounce around painfully in my skull. It's so shrill and high-pitched that it could be ultrasonic. In confusion and agony, I drop my phone and plaster my hands to my ears, protecting them from the abominable sound.

The bear shakes its head from side to side in the darkness, illuminated only by my discarded phone. It roars in retaliation, but a heartbeat later a great black shadow slams into the beast—knocking him sideways and across the cavern.

What the fuck was that? My guts twist inside me

as whatever it was that barreled into the bear shrieks again. My head swims, and I squeeze my eyes shut tight against the pain. I feel warmth trickle from my ears and between my fingers. I know with mortifying certainty that it's blood. Bones skitter in all directions as the two creatures fight, and I turn my face away, but then it hits me. Now is my chance. Maybe I can make a run for it while they're occupied?

Steeling my courage, I scramble to my feet and bolt haphazardly into the darkness, blind without my phone. It's live or die, I must take the risk. But my ears ring, and I have no idea in which direction I'm headed. I just run, hands outstretched before me, and pray to God that I make it out of here alive. Maybe West Virginia isn't so bad, after all.

Maybe I should count myself lucky to be breathing and able to stand on my own two feet? Maybe chasing a dream was the dumbest thing I ever did. But I don't have time to mull the thought over, because in the next two seconds my already dark and terrifying world comes to a bone-grinding halt. One moment I'm pelting through the inky gloom for my life, and the next—nothing.

Chapter Four

When I awaken pain greets me, ringing clarion clear in my ears. I wince, my hand flying to my head. "Fuck me," I breathe. Disoriented, it takes a moment for my situation to sink in and for me to remember just where I am. And a further several seconds to comprehend just what the fuck I'm looking at when I glance up, squinting in the firelight.

A tall shadow looms over me, wings flared, antennae erect. A scream dies on my lips as the figure squats down, and suddenly the nightmarish shape has a face, and I scramble backward on my ass for the second time, heart thumping in my chest like the drums of war. Big black, lidless eyes regard me with curiosity within a very otherwise humanlike face. My gaze roves over his body, drinking him in, every ounce of logic in my mind rejecting what my eyes are seeing.

His skin is as black as the night sky and has an iridescent sheen in the flickering light. The creature is lithe and athletically muscular, and his rippling ladder of abdominals makes my foggy brain swoon despite my sheer disbelief and terror. And as if my heart could bear another fright, my gaze drops between his thighs, and I almost die on the spot.

His cock is knotted like rope, with thick bulges every inch ... of which there are several. My stomach lurches and I raise my eyes to meet the creature's once more, before I find my voice. "You're the Mothman," I choke out.

"I am," he answers, his voice like silk and midnight.

"And you can talk," I gasp, my already fragile mind reeling.

"I can."

Chest rising and falling like I've just run a marathon, I lick my lips as I attempt to gather my thoughts. "This is impossible. You're an urban legend. A monster. A cryptid! You can't exist. I must be dead, or dreaming? Unconscious maybe?"

"I assure you, I am very much real, and you are very much alive."

Through the dull ache in my head, my thoughts scramble to make sense of this. "Oh my God. The bear," I breathe. "Holy shit, you saved me."

"Indeed, the bear is a friend of sorts. She keeps unwanted visitors at bay."

I swallow hard. "Your friend?"

"We are all animals, my pretty. We understand each other, though it takes time and patience. Something which humankind is sorely lacking."

"Is—" *I can't believe I'm going to ask this.* "Is the bear okay? I didn't mean to trespass. I was just hoping to get a photograph of the Falls. I thought the narrow path might lead to a beautiful view."

The Mothman snorts. "The bear is well. She was in her natural defensive bloodlust mode. It just took a little physical strength to remind her who is the alpha in these parts."

"I owe you my life," I say aloud, the realization dawning on me with startling clarity. "I'd be bear food right now if it wasn't for you."

"You do, and you would."

A tremor of apprehension ripples through me as he reaches out a strong hand toward me.

"Take my hand, brave girl, and I will show you how you can repay the favor."

I recoil, eyes wide, searching the unfamiliar earthen cavern around us for an escape. "I don't underst—"

"I think you do," interrupts the Mothman. "I have needs and desires. If you wish to live, you'll help me to fulfill and slake them."

My gaze falls back to the enormous knotty cock swollen between his muscular thighs and a part of me almost wishes the bear had succeeded. "I don't think that will fit."

"Oh, you'll be surprised what the female form can handle, my curvy mate."

"Mate?" I squeak.

The Mothman seizes me by my upper arms and lifts me to my feet, towering over me, his dark eyes gleaming. "On All Hallows' Eve I must deposit my eggs in a suitable womb. My cock aches with them."

"Eggs? Oh, Jesus, no." My legs give way beneath me, and it's only the Mothman's grip that keeps me upright.

"Each knot of my cock contains an egg, and all of them must find a home to be kept warm before they can be birthed and hatch."

I feel myself physically pale, like the blood has dropped out of me.

"Now, you can consent to being my mate or I'll let my friend pick up where she left off. The choice is yours."

Life or death. Vicious bear jaws tearing me apart, the air filled with my screams and the tang of my spilled blood. The unearthly pain of being eaten alive … or let the monster fuck me and live to see another day. What a choice. But it *is* a choice, no matter how horrific.

"So, what will it be?" he asks, black hair tumbling past his shoulders as his intense gaze bores into my soul.

"I don't know that I can stand," I whisper.

"You don't need to stand. You'll be on your back

and in my arms. I'll be all you need."

My mind swims and my tongue suddenly feels impossibly thick in my mouth, as if it's a dead weight made of stone that refuses to be moved.

"Consent, my lovely," says the Mothman. "You will enjoy our time together. You have my word. I can't promise the same of your time with my friend."

Visions of my limbs torn asunder and my face ripped off steal the spine out of me. I can't die yet. I have too much to live for!

"Yes," I whisper, though it's scarcely audible.

"You forget I have supernatural hearing, my little mate. Your consent is loud and clear."

I feel my sanity slipping, and fear eats away at whatever semblance of courage I have left.

In the next instant I'm thrown over the Mothman's shoulder and I feel jostled as he carries me somewhere new. As the last of my consciousness begins to fade, I can't help but notice the Mothman's tight black ass below me. He might be a terrifying monster with giant moth wings and segmented antennae. And he might fill me with his damn eggs. But there's no denying that the Mothman is fit as fuck, and almost beautiful in his own strange and ethereally cryptid kind of way...

Chapter Five

When I regain consciousness, I find myself sprawled on my back amongst a collection of soft blankets and pillows. Not what I expected. A fire burns in a pit nearby, and an intriguing array of trinkets and paintings lines the walls. Beyond the firepit, the cavern opens into eternity, the glittering stars go on forever, and the Black Water Falls National Park Forest sprawls below in all directions—like a sea of emerald-green bathed in shadow and moonlight.

And then the Mothman is down on his knees and between my legs, stalking over me. He lines up his mind-bending cock and begins to rub it up and down my slit. *My slit?* My leggings are gone, as are my boots. I'm naked from the waist down.

"Welcome back," says the Mothman.

I shudder at the feel of his flesh touching mine, but at the same time, I can't help but feel a twinge inside me. Whether I want to admit to it or not, there is something wickedly taboo and hot about the idea of being railed by a monster.

"I can smell your musk, little one," he says, interrupting my thoughts. "Do not be ashamed. I am built for mating. My form is as pleasing as can be to ensure successful breeding."

I can only stare down my body at him as he gently presses the head of his cock against me, increasing the pressure as he attempts to enter me.

"Wait," I gasp.

The Mothman glances up with his spectacular, insect-like eyes. They flash ruby-red in the firelight. Their beauty is mesmerizing.

"Do you have a name, besides 'Mothman', I

mean?"

"Curious," he muses. "I have been called a handful of things over the last couple centuries, but my true name is what I am and have always been. I am Omen."

My eyes widen. I should have known. "They say you appear before tragedy and life-changing events..." and that's the last coherent word to fall from my lips as Omen plows forward, sinking the first knot of his strange cock inside of my surprisingly wet cunt. A groan escapes me, and I instinctively claw at the blankets beneath me.

Omen smiles down on me, his mouth full of razor-sharp teeth. It's as beautiful as it is insane—the perfect expression of lunacy—and the very picture of Halloween.

My pussy reacts to the intrusion, clamping down around the knot as my back arches.

"You are so tight, my beauty," he says, before seizing my ankles and driving forward again.

A garbled moan of ecstasy burbles out of me, spilling like water from a fountain as his second knot stretches me wide again. The temporary burn of the stretch is everything. And despite every doubt and fear, my body acts of its own accord, pushing forward, desperate to consume him. Desperate for more. I've never been one to explore too broadly with my sexuality, having been preoccupied with merely surviving, but Omen's ropey, knotty cock feels better than any toy, or any man for that matter, that I've ever experimented with.

My hands stray to my breasts, and I rub my palms over my pert nipples. They feel alive with fire, as if charged with electricity, sensitive to even the most fleeting of touches. Adjusting myself on Omen's nest, I raise myself up on my elbows so that I can watch in erotic-fueled awe as the third delicious knot presses into my pussy. I bite down hard on my lip, accidentally drawing blood as it disappears inside of me. "Oh, God, yes," I whimper.

"Do you like my moth-cock, pretty? Do you think you can take it all? All seven of my knots?"

I don't know if I can, only God knows. But I sure as hell want to try. "Yes," I breathe, my gaze plaintive. "I want them all. It feels *so* good."

Omen pushes my legs together, and forward so that I'm forced onto the flat of my back once more. They press against me, folding me in half, and in one breathless moment another knot stretches and fills me.

My cunt locks down around him and I mewl at the incredible pressure inside of me.

"Count for me, my mate," croons Omen. "I want to hear you."

"Four," I gasp, my breathing heavy.

"You're juicy as fuck," he groans. "The last three are going to slide in so easily. And then, I'm going to fuck you—hard." His gorgeous, midnight-black form tenses as he presses forward.

"Five." I rake my fingers through my long ginger hair, grasping at fistfuls as I'm stretched again. "Six." One after the other his knots are buried inside my greedy cunt. *Oh God.* I feel indescribably full. I don't know if I can take any more. The last knot might be what breaks me. But there's no time to wonder on the fortitude of my pussy.

Omen hisses as the final knot is enveloped by my flesh.

"Seven!" I cry out, mortified and proud in equal measure.

"How does it feel to be the first woman to willingly take my monster cock, mate?"

Locked around him like a bitch in heat, my body

shudders with the exertion of containing him. "First?" I whisper.

Omen grins and it sends a shiver through my soul. "All have chosen to face my furry friend, rather than be joined with me."

My mind boggles. Omen might be the Mothman, an ancient cryptid monstrosity of the paranormal world, but there's no denying that he is mouthwateringly hot in a beastly and sinfully taboo way. How could anyone choose death at the dreadful maw and sinister claws of a bear, over being filled with his epic fucking knotted cock? *Those women must have been lunatics*, I reason, all thoughts of photography and New Orleans long forgotten.

"And now, I'm going to ruin you for mankind," says my strange and terrifying Mothman. "I'm going to fill you with my eggs, and you will be a mother of monsters—beautiful, frightful, and strong little cryptids who will make the wild forests of America their homes."

Chapter Six

Just when I don't think any of this can get weirder or more extreme, Omen scoops me up, still buried to the hilt.

"Wrap your legs around me, my lovely," he instructs, supporting my weight by groping my bare ass.

I wrap my legs around his hips, and my arms around his neck.

"Now, hold on. You're in for the ride of your life."

Impaled on several inches of monster cock, I can only do as he says. I have no idea what's to come. I can't even begin to guess.

Omen walks us past his warm, crackling firepit and to the edge of his cave. His taloned toes curl over the rock as I hang suspended over eternity.

"Oh my God. What the fuck!" I grip him more tightly. Horror consumes me at the thought of plunging to my death, skewered like a kebab on the trees far below.

"Calm yourself," says Omen directly into my ear. "I will not let you fall." And then he spreads his gorgeous, almighty moth wings, their patterned beauty flaring behind him. "We moths mate in the sky, beneath the beauty of the full moon."

My heart hammers in my chest, frantic to escape its ribbed cage and find safety within the rocky, solid foundations of the cavern. "Sky?" I squeak. Because knotted Mothman cock and birthing insect eggs clearly wasn't enough...

My heart plummets, a scream tearing from my throat as we suddenly drop, free-falling through the night toward the dark canopy below.

Omen's laughter fills the night, drowning out my

scream. Then his wings flare, catching the wind, and our descent becomes an effortless glide. Before I can find my voice again, the Mothman withdraws his cock, before slamming it back inside me.

My eyes roll back in my head, and I hang on for dear life, the crescents of my fingernails biting into Omen's black flesh.

And so, the fucking begins. With powerful, methodical thrusts, Omen plows my depths, his egg-filled knots plundering my wet, hungry cunt as he beats his wings, completely undeterred by my physical burden.

We rise and fall, soaring, and spiraling through the night. It's like a roller coaster without the rails. Like two animals locked in heat, our mating dance is beyond my control. Omen is the pilot, and I'm the passenger— the submissive partner to his dominant guidance and artful prowess.

Filled with unparalleled and intoxicating levels of adrenaline, as well as cock, I scream over and over again, until I taste blood. *Have I torn my bloody throat?* Even if I have, it's the least of my concerns. I blank in and out of consciousness. There's nothing but the sky and stars, and the all-encompassing radiance of the All Hallows' Eve moon one moment, and the very next the earth is almost upon us, ready to catch our fragile bodies with its hard, unforgiving, and crushing embrace.

And all the while Omen's knotted cock thrusts within me, hard, and bulbous.

My poor pussy gapes as he plunders me without remorse, lost to the frenzy of our mating. "Omen!" his name a desperate and strangled cry wrenched from my lips as we rise to greater heights. And for one breathless, heart-racing moment time falls away, and I feel if I just reached out and strained my fingers to their fullest extent, I could almost touch the moon.

But before I can dredge up the courage to relinquish my hold on the Mothman, we fall. The world rushes past us at impossible speed, and my hair flies, blocking my vision. I cling to Omen with all my strength in mortal terror as he fucks the shit out of me, his thrusts deeper, faster, and more frenzied.

Just as I think we're past the point of no return, and our flesh is destined to be united with the cruel, bone-crushing impact of the ground, he back-wings and glides, unleashing an unholy and hot torrent within me. His claws dig into my back, and he shrieks, the inhuman and godawful sound deafening me. One brutal thrust after another, his cock engorges, releasing all seven of his eggs inside me—a literal Mothman ovipositor.

My cunt instinctively clenches around him as the seventh and final egg releases.

Omen's cock feels impossibly huge, it's girth swells to fill my hole completely, sealing it shut so tightly that I couldn't release him even if I wanted to. No eggs will be falling out of me anytime soon. We're bound together like two mutts humping in the streets. Only we're hundreds of feet up in the air, and instead of creating cute little bastard puppies, we're creating monsters together. Monsters that are mine, as much as they are his.

The Mothman soars once more, wings pumping as he flies us back to his nest—his cozy, fire-heated cavern within the mountains of West Virginia. Before long, he touches down, and the world feels solid and secure once more. Omen carries me inside, his arms wrapped protectively around me. "We're home, mate," he whispers in my ear. "You did so well, my beauty. My eggs are inside you now, and we'll remain knotted until your womb accepts them."

My head spins, and I feel inexplicably exhausted,

like I've just run a marathon, or climbed a thousand stairs at speed. My body shudders around Omen's monstrous cock, and I sigh, just grateful to be back inside and on solid ground.

"We will sleep now," Omen whispers as he drops carefully to his knees on the nest of blankets and cushions. "And when you wake, we'll speak of what happens next."

Fatigue steals over me, and I relax, completely at ease as we lay down together, chest to chest, arms entangled around one another, him buried deep inside me. What could there possibly be to talk about? I'd just been mated by a monster.

Chapter Seven

Stretching my arms above my head, I yawn. I feel languid and warm. I'm free, I realize. Omen is nowhere to be seen. I tentatively reach down between my legs, my fingers grazing over my puffy pussy. *I* can't believe *I fit a fucking monster inside of me... Unreal!* And then my mind falls back to the eggs. "My God." I swallow the lump in my throat. "Eggs."

With trepidation building in me, I slowly trail my hands up and over my stomach, circling the subtle swell. No one would know anything was amiss if they looked at me. I'm on the curvier side of the scale already, with a distinct hourglass figure. My breasts are full, my ass sports some dimples, and my belly and thighs are pleasantly cushy—or so I've been told. *"More cushion for the pushin'*," one of my exes once said.

I shrug the thought away. *Fuck them.* Omen thinks I'm beautiful. Beautiful and brave, and strong enough to bear his offspring.

"I see you're awake," says the Mothman with a lopsided grin, a silver tray balanced on his splayed hand.

"How long have I been asleep?" I ask, rubbing my eyes as I sit up slowly.

"Just a couple of hours," he answers, crouching down before me. "Water?"

Grateful, I take the glass and swallow a sip. "Thank you. I didn't expect you'd have things like this."

"Home comforts?" he asks.

"Yes. I mean, you're a monster," I offer. "And you live in a deep, dark cave hidden in the mountains of the Black Falls. I didn't exactly imagine you'd have paintings, pillows, and glasses to drink from."

"How else would I live?" Omen laughs. "I might

be a monster, but we're not so different, pretty girl. I need to eat and sleep like everyone else."

"I suppose so," I say, draining the glass. "Did you steal it all?"

"I've acquired my homely comforts over many years. I have no need to steal from the living, when those who are dead leave what they have behind."

"And did you—" I purse my lips, then lick them. "Did you kill those people?"

Omen regards me curiously. "You truly know nothing of my kind, do you?" he asks. "I do not kill. I am a creature of prophecy and dark truths. My purpose is to foretell what is to come, and to procreate. No more and no less."

I can't prevent the easy smile from spreading my lips. "Well, you've managed to find a warm body to deposit your eggs. So, when do you foretell my future?"

"It doesn't work quite like that, I'm afraid. But I did foresee your coming."

"You did?" I ask, my brows furrowing.

"Think."

My frown deepens. *Think? On what?*

Omen reaches out and lays the flat of his palm against my forehead.

And suddenly I'm taken back in time, to earlier in the evening. I'm walking through the forest with my camera bag, and a glint of silver catches my eye. And then I'm returned to the present and Omen removes his hand.

"Oh my God!" I gasp. "The locket." I reach for the pendant nestled between my breasts. "You planted it, didn't you? As a marker? So that I'd follow the narrow path."

"Smart girl."

"I have a name, too, you know," I remark. "It's

Penelope, but most people just call me Penny."

"Well, Penny," says Omen, testing out my name for size. "My gift is unpredictable. I am but the means by which the truth of life reveals itself—like the paper upon which a letter is written. I foresaw that you were coming to the Falls, though I did not know why. I saw that you were beautiful, with a fine body. And I knew the true reason for your coming must be that you were my fated mate. So, I hung my locket for you to find—to tempt you toward my cave."

I gently pry the locket open with trembling fingers. "And this photo?" I query. "Who—"

"Who do you think?" says Omen.

"It's ... you?"

"I am not the only monster that was once a man, Penny. Many of us have been cursed to this life through no fault or choice of our own. I was once a young man with hopes and dreams before this fate befell me."

"What was your name before? When you looked like this?" I say, running my fingers over the old sepia portrait.

Omen's dark brow furrows now.

"You don't remember?"

"My old life feels distant and hard to grasp, like a dream fading in the morning light."

There's a tug on my heart, and I reach out to grasp his hand. "It's all right," I say. "It doesn't matter."

"I was called Nathanial," he says. "Nathanial Jacobson. I was the son of the town blacksmith."

Intrigued, I squeeze his hand. "What year were you born?" I ask.

"I was born in the year 1872 ... and I was twenty-five when my life changed forever. The turn of the century looked very different for me. Instead of assuming my father's business and settling down with a family, I found myself chosen by Fate. Exiled from humanity, I had no choice but to live as was intended—a recluse in the mountains, reborn with wings, antennae, bug eyes, and an entirely new color to blend in with the night."

"And you've been alone all this time?"

"Believe it or not, my brave Penny, there are not many who wish to believe in the existence of monsters, let alone desire to spend time with them. I'm an urban legend and myth. My place is in the shadows, beyond the awareness of humankind."

My lip trembles and my heart goes out to this beautiful man who had his life torn away by powers beyond his control. It suddenly makes my own dream of running away to New Orleans seem small and insignificant. Ridiculous, even. I'm alive and normal. I am not a spectacular beauty, and I scarcely get by paycheck to paycheck. But my life is my own, dictated by no one. Omen's life was stolen. *And he's alone.* No one deserves to be alone, especially not this terrifyingly beautiful and majestic creature.

"What if you didn't have to be alone?" I ask, a mad, impossible, and entirely new life plan brewing in my mind in an instant. "What if I stay with you even after our little monsters are hatched? What if I choose to truly be your mate—to stay with you … always?"

Chapter Eight

Omen's eyes flash red in the firelight, and he swallows hard, before rising to his feet. "You would give up your life to be with me?" he asks. "You'd forsake your family, friends, and your dreams? The modern conveniences? To live with me here in the forest?"

It sounds batshit mad. But somehow, I've never been more certain of anything in my life. Maybe West Virginia was never the problem? Maybe being alone in the world was. "My parents are dead, and I have no extended family or friends to speak of." I shrug. "As for dreams? They're just that—wistful wishes and empty hopes. Ever since my parents died all I've wanted to do was get out of this State. I thought that by being somewhere else I could start again. But now?" I stand, the fire of conviction blazing within me. "Now I think Fate brought us together for a reason. No one deserves to be alone, Omen. Not even a monster."

The Mothman turns his back on me, then his immense, patterned wings flare. "I yearn to accept such a possibility," he says, his voice wracked with emotion. "But I will not ask you to give up everything you know, the familiar and safe, for a life of darkness and seclusion. A beauty like you deserves the world."

I reach out and trail a hand down his muscular back, before embracing him from behind, my arms wrapping tightly around his waist. "Well, this is not your choice," I answer. "It's mine. If you'll love me and share your days and nights with me and our children, that is all I need."

Omen sighs, the sound like a breath of wind in the darkness. "I would have settled for offspring and let you free, Penelope."

"I am free," I say, a smile quirking my lips. "I'm freer in this moment, on this night, than I have ever been. I can't go back to what I knew, knowing you're here. I know it in my heart. I'd just come back. So, I'll just never leave in the first place." I gently release Omen. "Look at me."

Omen relaxes his wings and turns to face me.

"I want this. Unless you reject me and send me away, I will stay."

Omen catches my small face in his large hands. "I'd never send you away. I want to keep you."

"Then I'm yours."

In the next instant the Mothman stoops down to kiss me.

Despite his maw of sharp teeth, I have no fear. I know he won't hurt me—at least not in any way I'm not more than happy to endure. My hands wander between us, trailing down his abs, to the delicious V, and to his stiffening cock. I gasp, breaking our kiss to look down in wonder. "It's smooth!" I marvel.

Omen's lips are slack with lust. "Of course. My cock returns to a normal state when it's not engorged with eggs."

A wicked thought crosses my mind, and I lick my lips. "Well, then," I say. "I think it's my turn to show what I can do with this mouth of mine, and then maybe we can find another place for it..." With that, I turn him around and playfully shove him backward.

The Mothman's startlingly midnight-black skin has the most beautiful sheen, made more obvious by the combined luminance of the moon and the fire. He allows himself to fall into our eclectic nest, a broad and lunatic smile on his face.

"Just relax," I purr, getting down on my knees to crawl between his lithe and muscular thighs. "We'll take care of each other." I take his big, smooth cock in hand, and tucking my hair behind my ears, I bob forward, my hot mouth enveloping the tip.

Omen moans. "Sweet girl," he breathes. "The women of my time were not so forward."

I kiss the head of his cock, and glance up to meet his gaze. "Well, welcome to the twentieth century." I grin. "Women take what they want." And then I'm down again, my tongue swirling around his head and my other hand strokes his hard and impressive length. When he's thoroughly drenched in my saliva, I take him deeper and deeper, until he hits my gag reflex. I hold him hostage there as my throat spasms around him. If there's one thing I know, it's that I was born to deep-throat.

Again and again, I plunge him deep into my tender throat. His exclamations of ecstasy and his growly moans serve only to spur me on, encouraging me to greater efforts.

Then, without warning, he seizes the sides of my head, and begins to thrust his hips, fucking my face with a frenzied passion.

Relaxing my throat, I allow him to use me as he will, like a puppet of human flesh to be used and abused for pleasure. And as my eyes water, and I gasp around his cock, I feel whole. This strange, cursed monster is the missing piece of my life's jigsaw puzzle. Being his mate and having him claim my womb and face is erotic in ways I can't even begin to describe.

"Oh, fuck," Omen grates out as he continues. "Penny, I'm going to come."

With hot tears of exertion streaming down my face, I give his thigh a squeeze. My physical consent that it's all right. I brace myself as his thrusts become even more inhuman, and my face is all but mashed into his groin as he plunders me deep, seemingly desperate to spill his load directly into my stomach.

I clamp my lips around Omen's cock, creating a deliciously tight seal so that not a drop of his monstrous cum is wasted.

The Mothman releases my head, instead clinging to fistfuls of hair. "Yes, God, yes," he moans, and then his ultrasonic shriek overwhelms my senses—filling the cavern and echoing into the night.

I wanted so desperately to take him all, to swallow every last drop, but as I slam my hands down around my ears, and gasp in shock at the pain, his cum fills my mouth instead of my throat and I gag, coughing and spluttering in the most unsexy and unladylike way imaginable. "Holy shit," I choke as a fit wracks my body and my lungs burn. "I think I breathed in some cum!"

Chapter Nine

Omen stares at me.

I'm covered in thick, milky-white cum. I can feel it around my mouth, spilling down my chin, to drip splattered all over my black Halloween t-shirt. "Fuck. I sort of forgot about your climax screech," I say. "I normally pride myself on my deep-throat. I'm sorry I made a mess." I sigh.

"Are you serious, mate?" he asks, crawling forward onto his knees to touch my face tenderly. "Are you all right? I think I nearly drowned you!"

I can't help the snorting laughter that bursts out of me as I wipe my face on the back of my arm. "Yeah, you could say that. But I'm okay," I promise.

"Your clothes are ruined," he observes. "I'm afraid I don't have female attire here, but I could fashion you a dress of sorts. And your pants are over there where I left them."

I lean into his hand and smile. "That would be really nice. I'll have to go back into town and grab at least some of my things, so something warm would be great."

Omen rises and returns with a bowl of water and a cloth. "Here," he says. "Clean yourself up while I get to work."

The cold water is shockingly refreshing, and I hurry to wash away as much of Omen's seed as I can, carefully pulling my dirty shirt over my head so as not to get it in my hair.

Mothman returns a minute later with a warm tartan blanket with a hole cut out for my head. He slips it over my head, and then secures it around my waist with an old belt—most likely his from when he was still a young man.

Slipping into my pants, I re-lace my boots and straighten myself out, observing my reflection in a frosted glass mirror on the cave wall. "Well, that's as good as it's going to get," I surmise. "Thank you. I feel much better now."

"No," says Omen. "Thank you. I didn't hurt you, did I?"

I run my hands over his strong, warm chest. "Not a chance," I say. "I think I'm going to have to find my earmuffs, or pick up some earplugs, though, because that shriek of yours is kind of deafening."

Omen's eyes shine like blood-red rubies in the firelight. "It's a moth thing," he says by way of apology. "I wish I could remain silent, but my releases are so brutally intense, there's really no way I can."

A grin splits my face, and I stand on the tips of my toes as he leans down to kiss me. "Don't apologize for who and what you are, Omen. We can make this work. You'll see."

****

There're perhaps a few hours left of darkness when Omen carries me down the mountain, landing within the safety of the shadows of the tree line where my car is parked.

"Don't be long, mate," he coaxes, brushing my hair from my eyes. "I can't be seen during daylight hours."

"I'll be as fast as I can," I say, raising my gaze to his. "I'll have a few bags with me. Will you be able to carry that much?"

Omen's laughter is all the response I need.

"Okay, well. How will I let you know when I return?"

"I'll be watching," he promises. "I'll be waiting."

I lick my lips and nod. "See you soon." With that, I creep from the forest and hop into my little car that looks ridiculously like a pregnant roller skate. Careful to obey the traffic rules despite my excitement, I make it home to my rental in record time. I race around the house, filling my suitcase, and half a dozen bags with my belongings. Clothes, shoes, a sewing kit, my books and art supplies, as well as some practical necessities like toiletries, some cutlery, bowls, cups, towels, blankets, and a bunch of matches from my kitchen drawer.

Glancing around my ransacked home, I take a deep breath. *Am I really doing this?* I wonder to myself, heart racing. No more movies, no more electricity, no instant hot water. I'll have none of the modern conveniences I was raised with. *But what does that matter when you have the love of a monster?* a voice whispers deep inside. *It'll be like camping forever with the father of your monster babies!*

A smile twitches the corners of my lips and I nod to myself. Yep. I'm doing this. I have no idea what will happen once I'm gone. Will I be reported missing? Will debt collectors come looking for rent owed? How long until the town of Point Pleasant forgets I ever existed? Soon, I hope. I'll become a forgotten memory, the girl that wanted to get out, never to be seen again.

Stuffing my car, I lock the house behind me and leave the keys under the mat. It's time to go. In the distance, the faintest glow begins to peep above the horizon. The twilight hours are gone, and the dawn is upon us. Taking the fastest way I know back to Blackwater Falls State Park, I meet Omen in the same place.

Loading all my bags onto his arms, he kisses me on the forehead. "I'll be back for you shortly, mate. "I'll collect the bag you left by the cave, too."

"Thank you," I say, before he disappears into the last shreds of darkness that remain.

Leaving my car unlocked, with the keys in the ignition, I return to the trees to await my monstrous mate. "Well, this is it," I whisper to myself. "No more running. West Virginia is our home. Now, and for always."

Chapter Ten

As the dawn grows brighter, Omen retreats into a secondary den within our cave. The morning light hurts his eyes. I join him, filling the space with candles and cushions for comfort. "What do you eat, Omen?" I ask as I sink down beside him. "Do you even need to?"

Omen laughs, his bright teeth gleaming in the candlelight. "I do eat, though my diet is not like my insect kin. I hunt and eat game, like deer and rabbit, and sometimes ducks and wild geese. But right now? I'm going to eat you."

I gasp as I'm taken by surprise.

My devious Mothman stalks on top of me, tearing my clothes from my body with ease. Then he lowers his head to my chest, swirling his tongue around my hard nipples, before leaving a trail of hot kisses down my belly. He pushes my legs apart wide, dropping between my thighs, his lips tease my clit, his tongue snaking out to flick and suckle it.

I want to crawl out of my own skin. My God, that feels good! I bite my own fist as I moan, my other hand clutching at the blankets beneath me.

His tongue sinks inside me, pumping, deeper and deeper—impossibly deep.

I raise myself up on my elbows, eyes wide in the dim light. "Omen," I breathe. "How long is your tongue?"

Omen lifts his head, retracting his wicked tongue from my pussy, before revealing the impossible truth. It's obscenely long and thick, just like a popular comic book alien antihero. It's as unnerving as it is amazing.

I can feel myself growing wet just at the sight of it. "Oh my." *It's longer than his cock! Holy fuck!* And then all logical thought and contemplation leave me as in the next heartbeat that monstrous tongue is plunging back inside of me, probing depths that no man ever has before. Guttural moans tumble unchecked from my mouth as I experience the best fucking oral of my life. *Sweet Jesus.* He's ruined me. I'm his forever! Between his knotty cock and this magnificent tongue, I'm set for the rest of my days.

For how long this relentless clit-and-cunt torture goes on, I can't say. I lose track of how many times I come. There's just wave after wave of toe-curling ecstasy. Each merges into the next, until it seems my poor pussy is just trapped in one long, wickedly cruel orgasm. Tears leak from my eyes and soon I'm begging him to stop. I feel jelly-legged, or like a wrung-out towel. I've got no more energy. He's literally licked, sucked, and tongue-fucked it out of me.

"Last time, my mate. Come for me," growls Omen, before slapping my pussy as if it were an ass. I'm so riled and strung out that the sharp sting does it for me, and I scream out, my cunt spasming uncontrollably as I writhe on our makeshift nest like a cut snake.

Omen sits back on his haunches, just watching me, clearly satisfied with a job well done. "Are you happy, mate?" he asks.

I rake my fingers through my hair and stare at the cavern roof above, huffing out a dramatic breath. "I have never experienced anything like that before. I don't think I could stand right now, even if I wanted to. I'm fucking well fucked. Thank you."

Omen grins. "Good. I'll steal the legs from you at least twice a day from now until our end."

I roll over onto my side and snuggle up. "Sounds too good to be true."

My Mothman gently lays a heavy wool blanket

over me, then spoons in behind me, wrapping a protective arm over me. "For now, let's rest," he says, his breath hot on my ear. "But I'm going to go hunting once it gets dark. Sleep well, Penny. When I return, I'll rustle up something for you. You'll no doubt be ravenous when you wake." He chuckles.

"Mmm," I moan softly. "A hot meal would be amazing." Fatigue begins to wash over me, tugging mercilessly at my eyelids. "Thank you, mate," I whisper, before giving into the promise of sex-satiated oblivion.

****

The smell of roasted game reaches my senses and I stir, stretching and yawning. I place my flat palm against my stomach. It feels slightly more firm than usual, which isn't surprising, given my womb is currently gestating seven eggs. "I'm going to take care of you, little ones," I coo, rubbing circles on my belly. "And your father will protect us all."

Fumbling through one of my bags, I locate my fluffy bathrobe and shrug it on, then wrap the fabric belt around my waist and secure it with a casual knot. Rubbing the sleep from my eyes I wander out into the central cavern where the firepit burns cheerfully. "Oh my God, I breathe. "It's dark. I slept all day?"

The stars shimmer beyond, as Omen rises from beside the pit, a plate of steaming roasted meat in hand. "You did," he says. "It's a few hours after sunset. I didn't have the heart to wake you."

I yawn again and plonk myself down on a cushion facing the incredible view. "Is that for me?" I ask, hunger stirring in my belly. "It smells delicious. What is it?"

"Rabbit," says Omen, dropping down beside me. He passes me the plate with a smile. "Eat up, mate. Incubating our babies is going to take a lot out of you, but I'll keep you fed and safe. I promise."

The meat is crispy on the outside, and perfectly succulent inside. I carefully pick at a piece, burning my fingertips, but I'm so hungry I don't care. Piece after piece, I devour my portion, then suck my greasy fingers clean. "Thank you, Omen. That was delicious. I swear the meat just melted in my mouth."

"What can I say?" says the Mothman. "I'm a sexy monster that can cook."

"You can say that again," I agree, leaving the plate on the ground before pouncing on him. "I never imagined I could be so lucky," I say, pleased to feel Omen's stiff black cock against me. "How about I steal the legs from *you*?" I challenge, before pushing him back and positioning myself directly above him.

"You can try," he counters as his strong hands take hold of my waist.

Taking his cock in my hand, I rub it against my already wet slit, dipping his head just inside my cunt, before removing it and sliding it back. Holding my breath, I ease my weight down and his cock punctures my puckered, tight ass. *My God, he's huge.*

A hiss escapes him, and his eyes gleam with feral lust.

I take him all the way, until I'm sitting on him, flush against his firm sac. Biting my lip, I offer him a seductively playful smirk. "You bet your ass I'm going to try."

As the moonlight pours into our cozy mountaintop cavern, bathing us in its mystical light, I feel empowered beyond my wildest and most lunatic desires. I'm going to fuck the Mothman's bloody brains out! No regrets. I don't need photographs. I'm going to live every moment, every day like it's my last.

The End

EVERNIGHT PUBLISHING ®

www.evernightpublishing.com